IRONSIDE

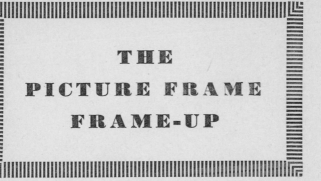

THE PICTURE FRAME FRAME-UP

Authorized Edition

by WILLIAM JOHNSTON

Illustrations by LARRY FREDERICK

WHITMAN PUBLISHING DIVISION
WESTERN PUBLISHING COMPANY, INC., RACINE, WISCONSIN

CONTENTS

1 Taking Pictures for Profit

FORTUNATELY, the private office of Gerard Mehl, owner of Mehl, Inc., one of San Francisco's most respected art auction houses, was fairly large. At the moment it had to accommodate not only Mehl and two of his employees, but also Robert T. Ironside, the city's legendary chief of detectives, now working out of the police commissioner's office on special assignment; his two assistants, Detective Sergeant Ed Brown and Policewoman Eve Whitfield; and his aide, Mark Sanger.

Ironside, big and bulky in the wheelchair to which

9

an attempt on his life had confined him, concentrated his attention on the two Mehl employees: Frank Buckley, the older man and driver of the Mehl, Inc. truck, and Arnold Jones, his helper. Gerard Mehl, middle-aged, bald, and small, sat at his desk looking annoyed, drumming his fingers nervously. Ed Brown, tall and attentive, stood near the doorway. Eve Whitfield sat in a chair near the corner of Mehl's desk, her head slightly tilted, her attractive features forced into a speculative frown. Mark Sanger, dark-skinned, trimly built, and constantly watchful, stood a few feet behind Ironside's wheelchair, leaning casually against a wall.

"Were you aware of the value of the paintings, Mr. Buckley?" Ironside asked, his tone moderate and amiable.

Although the office was air-conditioned, Buckley, a big man with thick, graying hair, was perspiring freely. "I didn't know for sure, Chief," he replied. "A guy can guess, though, you know. I see that mansion and the guards at the gate, and I can figure it out pretty much."

"Frank," Gerard Mehl said, "I think I mentioned to you that the Tuck collection had — has — a value of several million dollars. That, as I recall, was my exact phrase — 'several million dollars.' "

"Yeah, I guess you did say that." Buckley nodded. He wiped his upper lip with the back of his hand. "Right now I'm a little mixed up. I never lost nothing so important before."

"Correction," Gerard Mehl said testily. "You didn't

10

lose the paintings, Frank. They were stolen. We all know what you mean, but let's not give the insurance company any excuse for accusing us of laxity."

"Right — stole," Buckley quickly agreed.

Ironside turned his attention to Buckley's helper, Arnold Jones. Jones was in his early twenties. He had an open, innocent-looking face.

"Mr. Jones, where was it you said you stopped on the way from the Tuck mansion back to the auction house?"

Jones looked suddenly startled.

"We didn't stop no place, Chief," Buckley said.

Ironside smiled fleetingly. "Please, Mr. Buckley. Allow Mr. Jones to make his own answers."

"That's right — what Frank says," Jones affirmed. "We didn't stop nowhere."

Ironside made a soft, sighing sound. "Well . . . as they say in the detective stories, perhaps we'd better start at the beginning." He nodded to Buckley. "Frank, you're the spokesman, apparently. So let's have it."

"I told Mr. Mehl," Buckley replied. "Maybe he could tell it better than me."

Ironside shook his head. "You were there, Frank. You tell it."

Buckley shifted his position. "Well, yesterday we got instructions from Mr. Mehl. He said to take some crates and the packing stuff and tomorrow — today, that is — to drive out to the Tuck place and pick up these paintings — fifty-seven of them. And that's what we did."

11

"What time this morning did you arrive at the Tuck mansion?" Ironside asked.

"Nine o'clock, like the instructions. There's a big iron fence all around the place, and the guard at the gate let us in. Mr. Tuck was right there to meet us."

"David Tuck, himself?" Ed Brown asked. "You mean he was waiting at the gate?"

"At the house — the main house," Buckley replied, shaking his head. "The guard said where to drive, and when we got there Mr. Tuck was waiting, and he took charge. He showed us this room where he had the paintings stored — the place is so big, you know, it must have a thousand rooms — then he waited there while we got the crates and brought them up. He was with us every minute, except when we was lugging them crates up, and then later when we was taking them back down with the paintings in them."

Ironside turned to Gerard Mehl. "Is it customary for the owner to preside over the crating?"

Mehl shrugged. "Sometimes; sometimes not. It all depends. The paintings — as I think it's been established now — are worth several millions. And Mr. Tuck is a —" he was seeking the right word — "a careful man. There are certain things, especially things concerning great sums of money, that I imagine he prefers to . . . ahh. . . ."

"Stay on top of," Ironside said, supplying the phrase and at the same time switching his attention back to Buckley. "Mr. Tuck stayed with you while you crated

12

the paintings, you say. Then what?"

"He didn't just stay there," Jones put in.

"That's right," Buckley agreed. "He wanted to show us exactly how to do it. Like Mr. Mehl says, he's very careful. Not that we needed no telling, but we got it, anyway."

"And then?"

"Then, from there, after we had all the paintings packed, we went up to his office," Buckley continued. "It was on a floor up above — or maybe two floors. We went up by elevator, so it's hard to remember. He had a receipt there that his secretary or somebody had typed up, and he had me sign it that I had responsibility for the paintings now; then we went back down."

"That was an error," Gerard Mehl said, "but it's not particularly important."

"An error how?" Ironside asked.

"Frank should have put the crates on the truck before he signed the receipt. As it was, the paintings were still in the house; he didn't have possession of them. But I don't think it's really important."

Ironside thought for a second, then shrugged and resumed the questioning. "With Tuck watching — or directing — you crated the paintings, then took an elevator to his office and signed the receipt. Did he stay in his office?"

"Oh, no," Buckley replied. "He took us back to the room. He took us back, and he stayed right with us until we had the crates in the truck and we left."

"Did he see you to the gate and out?"

"No, he didn't go to the gate with us. He stayed at the door, and we drove on to the gate. That's the last we saw of him, when we left him at the house."

"We can assume, then," Eve said, "that he relinquished interest in the paintings at that point."

"Right now we can assume nothing," Ironside said crisply. He addressed Buckley once more. "You're sure, now, that you made no stops between the Tuck estate and here? Do you smoke? Perhaps you stopped for a pack of cigarettes."

Buckley shook his head.

Ironside looked at Jones. "Weren't you going to say something a second ago, Jones, about stopping?"

There was no hesitation on Jones's part this time. "We drove straight through, sir, right from the house to here," he said. "The only stop we made was at the gate, where the guy let us out."

"No traffic lights?"

"Well, sure, we hit some lights," Jones replied.

"Chief," Gerard Mehl asked with a smile, "does it strike you as possible that fifty-seven crated paintings could be removed from a locked truck while it stopped at a traffic light?"

Ironside smiled, too. "Just questioning Mr. Jones's statement that no stops were made," he said. "I thought that if he remembered one — or two — he might remember another."

"Traffic lights, sure," Jones said. "But other than

14

that, we didn't make no stops."

"Nevertheless, you insist that when you got here and opened the truck the paintings were gone?"

Gerard Mehl leaned forward. "Just a second, now, Chief. You're putting the wrong interpretation on this. The paintings were gone, yes. But the crates were still there. We're not saying — not specifically — that the theft was accomplished while the truck was en route. We haven't the faintest idea how this happened. No theory at all."

"We know *we* didn't do it, though, Arnold and me," Buckley said defensively, nodding toward his helper.

"Who accused you, Frank?" Ironside asked, studying him interestedly.

"Nobody. I'm just saying."

Ironside motioned for Buckley to continue the story.

"We got here and unloaded the crates," he responded. "I called Mr. Mehl, and he come back to the storage room, and we started taking the wrappings off. That's when we found out we didn't have nothing. Empty crates, that's all."

"Magic," Eve said.

"I gave up believing in magic when I was ten," Ironside said. "A magician told me he was going to pull a rabbit out of a hat, and he got a dove. The rabbit fell out of his sleeve later, when he was looking for a dove in his hip pocket."

"That's a terrible thing, to be disillusioned at ten," Eve said.

15

Gerard Mehl cleared his throat. "We were discussing paintings, I believe."

"Paintings that disappeared, as if by magic," Ironside reminded him. "But you have no theory on that, you say. Fifty-seven crates, each crate containing a valuable painting, are loaded aboard a truck. The rear doors of the truck are locked. The truck sets out for a drive of . . . of how many miles?"

"Sixty-some," Buckley replied.

"Of sixty-some miles. En route it stops only for red lights. Then, when it reaches its destination and the crates are opened, they're found to be empty." He snorted. "I take it back; I believe in magic again."

"I know it sounds crazy, Chief," Buckley said, "but that's how it happened."

"How was traffic?" Ironside asked him. "Fast or slow?"

"Medium. It was early afternoon. Pretty smooth sailing, I'd say."

"What would *you* say?" Ironside asked Jones.

"The same."

Ironside nodded. "I expected that." He addressed Buckley again. "All right, the traffic was medium, and it took you how long to travel from there to here?"

"Hour and a half, maybe; something like that," Buckley replied. "When we got back into the city, you know, we couldn't keep up the speed. Anyway, I wasn't paying much attention. How did I know it would be important how long the trip was?"

"I'd like to know your route — exactly," Ironside said. "Could you write it down for me, please?"

"Well . . . yeah, I guess."

Gerard Mehl handed Buckley a pad and a pencil, and Buckley began detailing the route the truck had taken from the Tuck mansion to the auction house.

"Since you no longer have the paintings to auction off —" Ironside began, speaking to Mehl.

"Correction, Chief," Mehl broke in. "I have not at any time had the paintings. They did not reach here. I understand what you meant when you said that, but just for the record I want to make it clear that I have never had possession of the paintings."

"Yes, of course. Since there'll be no auction, you'll obviously lose the commission on the sales. But is that all? Or did you have some additional stake in this?"

"It won't do my public image any good," Mehl replied. "But then, my reputation is such that it can take a much more severe battering than this and survive."

"I was thinking about money," Ironside said.

"No. I'll lose the commission — that is, assuming that the paintings are not found and therefore the auction does not come off. But otherwise I'll suffer no financial loss."

"And Mr. Tuck?" Ironside asked.

"The paintings are insured," Mehl replied. "He'll sustain a loss, but — Well, I think you'd better discuss that aspect of it with Mr. Tuck."

"The heavy loser, then, will be the company which

insures the paintings?" Ironside asked.

"That would be my assumption," Mehl answered.

Buckley handed Ironside a page from the pad. "This is it," he said. "It's not much; it was a straight drive, about."

"Thank you, Frank," Ironside replied. "Those are all the questions I have at the moment. I may want to talk to you again, however." He turned to Jones. "And thank you, too," he said.

Buckley and Jones left the office. When they had gone, Ironside sat for a moment studying the page of notepaper Buckley had handed him. Then he focused his attention on Mehl.

"Is Frank Buckley an art fancier?" he inquired.

Gerard Mehl hunched his shoulders, expressing minor hostility to the question. "Frank Buckley wouldn't know a Picasso from a Tommy Ryan," he replied. "But I didn't hire him to be an art expert. I hired him to build and haul crates, and he's very good at that. He's also totally trustworthy. Frank has been with me for close to five years, and in that time he's handled millions upon millions of dollars in paintings without ever losing a penny's worth."

"Whoever figured out this heist didn't do it overnight," Ironside said. "Maybe it took him 'close to five years' to work it out."

Mehl shook his head. "Frank is above suspicion."

"And Jones?"

"He's been with me about a month," Mehl replied.

18

"He's had odd jobs before. I can't tell you a great deal more about him."

"We'll want a list of your employees," Ironside said. "Everybody will be checked out. But you could save us some time if one of them, in your estimation, might be more likely to —"

"I trust them — all of them," Mehl said. "I wouldn't have them working for me if I didn't."

"Uh-huh," Ironside grunted, unimpressed with the logic. "Mr. Mehl," he said, "several million dollars in paintings went into that truck at the Tuck estate, and, at this point, they're missing. Now, according to their own story, only Buckley and Jones had any contact with the paintings while they were en route. If they didn't stop on the way, then the explanation for the puzzle must be here at the auction house, wouldn't you say?"

Mehl frowned. "I wouldn't say," he answered. "I'm not a detective."

Ironside smiled fleetingly. "Thank you for your help," he said. He motioned, and Mark moved in behind him, following a step behind as Ironside wheeled his chair toward the door. "By the way," Ironside added, "you said that Frank Buckley wouldn't know a Picasso from a Tommy Ryan. I know a little bit about art, but I've never heard of Tommy Ryan. Who is he?"

"My twelve-year-old nephew," Mehl replied, rising from his seat behind his desk. "He paints by number."

Ironside stopped and stared evenly at Mehl for a second. Then, without comment, he wheeled himself toward the doorway, where Ed Brown was holding the door open for him.

"Who topped who?" Mark asked as he, Ironside, Eve, and Ed proceeded along the corridor toward the exit.

"He cheated," Ironside complained gruffly. "Ringing in twelve-year-old nephews is cheating of the worst kind."

"Does that make him our prime suspect?" Eve asked.

"It certainly doesn't help his cause any," Ironside replied. "But I think we'll need a bit more evidence than the obvious fact that he cheats at one-upmanship."

Mark opened the exit door, and Ironside wheeled himself through, followed by Eve and Ed. It was late afternoon, and the sidewalk was crowded with homeward-bound pedestrians.

As they cleared the doorway, Ed Brown suddenly sprinted forward, without a word of explanation, and raced through the crowd, headed in the direction of the old paddy wagon that Ironside now used for transportation.

"Mark — back him up!" Ironside snapped.

Mark bolted after Ed Brown, swivel-hipping smoothly between the obstructing pedestrians like a nimble-toed quarterback making his way through an attack of opposing linemen.

"What was it? Did you see?" Ironside demanded of Eve as they set out to catch up with Ed and Mark.

"I didn't see a thing," she replied. "Did you?"

Caught in a squeeze between a lady with a poodle

and a delivery boy with a nose-high stack of packages, Ironside answered with a disgusted mutter.

When they reached the van, Mark was behind the wheel checking the switches. The headlights blinked on, then off.

"What's this all about?" Ironside asked, addressing Ed, who was standing on the sidewalk.

"I spotted somebody in the front seat," he replied. "I didn't get here fast enough to catch him, though."

Ironside shouted up to Mark. "Get down from there!" he commanded. "Our visitor might have been planting an explosive. Don't touch one more switch! You could blow us from here all the way to L.A."

Carefully Mark climbed down. "I know a bird in L.A. who'd be happy to see me," he said.

"In small parts?" Ironside asked. "Get a flashlight and check all the dark corners — under the control panel, under the hood, under the chassis. Check it out good. The life you save may be your own."

"Right," Mark nodded.

Ironside turned back to Ed. "How close a look did you get? Did you recognize him?"

Ed shook his head. "Just as we stepped out onto the sidewalk," he said, "I saw movement down here, a reflection on the windshield. It looked like somebody in the front seat. Maybe I was wrong."

Mark, who had gotten a flashlight and had started to crawl into the space below the control panel, suddenly backed out, holding a sheet of paper.

21

"Here's your bomb," he said to Ironside.

Ironside scowled at the message that was printed on the page of notepaper:

STAY AWAY FROM THIS CASE

"You weren't wrong. We *did* have a visitor, apparently," Ironside said.

"Tommy Ryan, I'll bet," Eve said, looking over Ironside's shoulder at the note. "That looks like a kid's trick."

"And reads like it," Ed added.

Ironside nodded agreement. "A kid — or a man with limited writing ability," he said. He took out a piece of notepaper from his jacket pocket and held it up beside the message found in the front compartment of the van. "Frank Buckley printed this other one," he said. "As you can see, it's the route I had him write down for me."

"That's the same printing, all right," Eve said.

"Shall I pick him up?" Ed asked.

Ironside pondered a moment, then shook his head. "He's got our hook," he said. "Let's let him run with it for a while."

Ed Brown looked at Eve, then at Mark, then back to Ironside. "May I ask why? There's no question in my mind that he wrote that threat."

"Threat?"

"Well, that's what he meant: Stay away from this case, or else."

"We don't know that," Ironside replied. "That's only your guess, Ed. Think about it, though. If Buckley did leave this note, wasn't it a pretty dumb move? How could I possibly miss the fact that it was his printing, already having a sample of it?"

"That's dumb," Mark said.

"But the man who planned and executed this theft, the lifting of those paintings — was he dumb? Hardly. So either Buckley did not do both — leave the note and lift the paintings — or Buckley is a lot smarter than he appears to be, or Buckley is a lot dumber than he appears to be and is being used by somebody with a lot of brains, or — Well, anyway, the list of possibilities could go on and on."

"There's another thing, too," Eve said. "I got the impression that Frank Buckley is aware of the Chief's reputation. And if he is, he knows that leaving a note telling Robert T. Ironside to stay away from a case is the one thing in this world that would *not* keep him away from the case. So explain that."

Ed Brown pulled at an ear. "I'm beginning to suspect that this isn't going to be a simple, ordinary, everyday stolen-property beef," he said.

Ironside laughed. "With several million dollars at stake? I want you to go back to the auction house," he said to Ed, "and get that list of employees from Gerard Mehl. Every name on it — check it out. Frank Buckley's name, though, especially. However, don't give the other ones a fast shuffle just because you're convinced that

Buckley is our man. That might be exactly what somebody wants us to think." A sudden thought occurred to him, and he emphasized its importance by poking the air with a finger. "Gerard Mehl — check him out thoroughly, too. Put his name through the file, and talk to some of his competitors and a few of his employees."

"He's a loser," Mark said. "You said it yourself: If there's no auction, there's no commission for him."

"Which would you rather have," Ironside asked, "the commission on the sale of several million dollars' worth of paintings or the several million dollars' worth of paintings themselves?"

"I get the point," Mark nodded.

Ed left to return to the auction house. Using the lift, Mark raised Ironside, wheelchair and all, and Eve into the van. After closing the rear doors, he returned to the driver's compartment.

"Where to?" Mark asked, speaking through the opening to the rear.

"The Tuck estate — where else?" Ironside replied. "The scene of the crime is always the best place to find the criminal, isn't it?"

"The scene of the crime could be anywhere between Tuck's place and the auction house," Mark reminded him.

"On the way, I'll keep a sharp lookout," Ironside assured him.

Mark started the motor, and a few seconds later the van pulled out into traffic.

24

"Since we're on our way to see him, wouldn't it be a good idea to tell Mr. Tuck we're coming?" Eve said.

"You think he might want to bake a cake?"

"No, but is it all right just to drop in on very, very, very, very rich people?"

"It is if you're the police and the circumstance is right," Ironside answered. "But. . . ." He motioned toward the mobile telephone.

Eve made the call. When she hung up, she was smiling mischievously. "Did you get all that?" she asked Ironside.

"As I understand it, *my* private secretary and David Tuck's private secretary have reached an agreement on the time and place for the two great men to meet. Why did you tell her you were my private secretary?"

"If he can have a private secretary, you can, too," Eve said belligerently. "You deserve it more than he does, anyway. Anybody can be rich, but how many people can be Robert T. Ironside?"

"I'd be more interested in that question if you re-phrased it," Ironside said. "It should be: Anybody can be rich, but how many people can be rich and be David Tuck, to boot. He's not your ordinary, everyday — as Ed would put it — multimillionaire, you know."

"I know. He's self-made."

Ironside shook his head. "That doesn't describe him. There are plenty of self-made multimillionaires. But David Tuck . . . . Well, he has a flair, a way of doing things; there's a kind of excitement —"

25

"Do you know him?" Eve interrupted, surprised.

"I've never met him. But I've read about him, of course."

"So have I. And I had that general impression, too, I suppose. But you sound like . . . well, like a fan."

"Maybe I am." Ironside smiled. "I admire men who have a certain presence, who do things with a certain confidence and expertise — as I said, men with a flair."

"I wonder if David Tuck does."

"Does what?"

"Admire men with a flair."

"I suppose so," Ironside said. "There's a little self-admiration in all of us."

"You two ought to be crazy about each other." Eve grinned.

2 The Ambiguous Connoisseur

As THE CONVERTED paddy wagon left the city and turned onto the parkway that would take it toward the Tuck estate, Ironside fell silent. His expression became forbidding and deeply thoughtful.

It was clear to Eve Whitfield that the case had become a challenge to Ironside. When the commissioner had called him in on it, she knew he had expected it to be no more than a routine task of hunting down a fairly imaginative, but garden-variety, thief. Now, however, he was baffled. No lead seemed even promising to him. He was, in effect, enjoying himself thoroughly.

Ironside took out the note that had been left in the front seat of the van and studied it. Then he compared it with the set of directions that Buckley had printed on the sheet of notepaper. Finally, shaking his head, he put both pieces of paper back into his pocket.

"Everything points to Buckley," Eve said. "Why are you so sure he didn't do it?"

"I'm *not* sure," Ironside replied. "I'm very doubtful, however. The theft was cleverly planned — and Buckley is not clever. Or, if he is, he certainly has me fooled." He called to Mark. "How much longer?"

"A few more minutes," Mark responded.

"I wonder if David Tuck will live up to his publicity," Eve said.

Ironside shrugged. "What are you expecting?"

"Oh, a kind of modern-day swashbuckler . . . a pirate in a gray flannel suit."

"That may not be too far from it," Ironside replied. "He's made his money, you know, not by managing companies, but by raiding them and merging them. I suppose he's a pirate — in a sense — but a modern pirate, as you say. He doesn't plunder. He makes his conquests keep working for him."

Eve frowned. "How, exactly?"

"He'll take over a company that's going downhill. Then he puts in new management and makes the company start paying off again."

"What's the matter with that?"

28

"It depends on who you are." Ironside smiled wryly. "If you're part of the old management, and you get kicked out, it looks like a dirty trick."

"Oh." She frowned again. "You know, if you hadn't joined the force, you might have become a swashbuckler yourself. There's a certain type, and you're it — you and David Tuck, apparently."

"There are those who will tell you that joining the force did not interfere in the least with my becoming a swashbuckler," Ironside returned with a smile.

"I think they're right. And if I ever need any swashes that need buckling, you're the one who'll get all my business."

"I think I'm already getting —"

Mark's voice from the driver's seat interrupted. "It's right up ahead," he announced.

Ironside and Eve moved forward to where they could look out the front window. The Tuck estate was to the left of the parkway, situated on a high rise that was thick with trees. They could see the spires of what appeared to be a Gothic castle.

"Straight out of Hollywood!" Mark exclaimed.

"Not quite," Ironside said. "That castle was shipped over here from Europe about fifty years ago by one of the railroad tycoons."

"Shipped over?" Eve asked incredulously.

"In sections," Ironside explained, "and then reassembled. David Tuck bought it about five years ago. He said he needed it as a setting for his paintings."

29

The van turned off the parkway, followed another main route for a few hundred yards, then, at a sign, turned again and followed a narrow, graveled path to a high iron gate. A guard, dressed in slacks and a T-shirt and carrying a shotgun, stepped from a small sentry house. He spoke with Mark for a moment, then unlocked the gate and allowed the van to pass.

The drive from the gate to the main building took a few minutes; the road was narrow and overhung with trees and vines. They were suddenly met with a burst of sunshine, however, and they found themselves in the spacious, open plaza that surrounded the castle. The castle itself loomed before them like an ancient and angry monarch.

"Impressive — in fact, a little scary," Eve said.

"What scares me is the thought of getting lost in there," Mark said. "It must have a thousand rooms."

"Not quite," Ironside said. "Close to a hundred, though."

"How do you know so much about David Tuck and his castle?" Eve asked.

"He's always interested me," Ironside replied. "When I read something about him — or his castle — I file it away in my memory, that's all."

The van stopped at the main entrance, and a middle-aged man, a servant, appeared. He, too, spoke with Mark, then disappeared back into the castle.

"He's announcing us." Mark smiled as he operated the mechanism that lowered Ironside and his wheelchair.

The entry hall was at least two stories high and as large as a good-sized apartment. It was dimly lighted, but, looking up, they could see heavy wood beams and hand-wrought iron chandeliers overhead. The floor was of solid stone, and the walls were hung with shields and swords.

"I still say it came straight from Hollywood," Mark commented.

A middle-aged woman approached them from out of the dimness. She introduced herself as Mrs. Alcorn, then led them to an elevator and escorted them to the third floor. There the lighting was somewhat better.

"I see Mr. Tuck didn't lose all his paintings," Ironside said, indicating the pictures that were hung in the corridor along which Mrs. Alcorn was leading them.

"You'll have to discuss that with Mr. Tuck, sir," she answered.

There was a small office beyond the heavy-looking open door at the end of the corridor. Presumably it was Mrs. Alcorn's. Another door led to David Tuck's quarters. His office was huge, with thick, Oriental-style carpeting and towering, arched windows that looked out and down on a tangle of unkempt garden.

"Chief Ironside," Tuck said, rising from behind a mammoth carved desk that supported a forest of telephones. He was a big man — Ironside's size — with thick shoulders and large hands. He was smiling slightly as he strode forward to meet his visitors. The smile remained fixed as Ironside introduced the others.

31

Tuck dismissed Mrs. Alcorn, then returned to his desk. A moment after he seated himself, one of the phones rang. He picked it up, listened, then shook his head and said, "No — and no more calls for a while, please." Hanging up, he said to Ironside, "You have my full cooperation — my time and my attention. Have you figured out yet how they did it?"

"Is that a specific 'they' or just 'they' in general?" Ironside asked.

"I was referring to the drivers."

"Buckley is the driver; Jones is his helper," Ironside said. He shook his head. "No, we haven't figured out yet how they did it, Mr. Tuck. We haven't —"

"Call me Dave."

Ironside grunted, then went on. "In fact, we haven't even decided that they *did* it. What information do you have that makes you so positive?"

"From what Gerard Mehl told me, who else could have done it?"

"An excellent question —" Ironside smiled — "as a matter of fact, the exact question that we're trying to get an answer to right now. So if you could start from the beginning and tell us, step by step, everything that led up to the theft. . . ."

David Tuck's story was a repeat of the story told by Buckley and Jones. The two men had arrived that morning. Tuck had met them, had directed the packing, then had taken them to his office to sign the receipt. After putting the crates into the truck and locking the rear door, they had driven off toward the city.

"There are a hundred places where they could have stopped," he said.

"Perhaps not a hundred — but several," Ironside admitted. "I didn't mean to imply that Buckley and Jones are above suspicion. But it's necessary, of course, to make a thorough investigation, and that requires collecting all the information we can get. I understand that the paintings were insured."

Tuck laughed. "I'm a terrible host," he said. "There's no need for us to sit here in this office. There *are* other, more comfortable places, and perhaps some refreshments besides."

"This will be fine, right here," Ironside replied. "Now . . . the paintings . . . they *were* insured, weren't they?"

Tuck smiled broadly. "Am *I* a suspect, Chief?"

"Not necessarily," Ironside replied evenly. "It's simply necessary, as I said, to collect *all* information."

Tuck got up and walked to one of the windows. "Can you see the garden?" he asked. "It's a mess, a jungle. I keep it that way — a bit of symbolism. The affairs of man get that way when they're not tended. All the details — all the tiny details — require attention. You understand that, don't you, Chief?"

Ironside was silent for a moment; then he nodded. "Yes, I suppose so."

"I can see that you do," Tuck said. "And that's why you have a reputation for winning. You pay attention to details." He faced his visitors. "I attend to the details, too," he continued. "That's the basis for whatever success I've had."

"Well, that's interesting, of course," Ironside said, "but it doesn't quite answer my question."

"Oh, I wasn't answering your question. I was responding to your suspicion. You've heard, I assume, that I sometimes play a . . . a dirty game." He shook his head. "It isn't true. I have, I'll admit, clipped a few men from behind, but only to avoid being clipped from behind myself. When the game is played by the rules, then that's the way I play it."

"And vice-versa?"

"And vice-versa," Tuck confirmed.

"As I said a moment or so ago, that's very interesting," Ironside said. "It wasn't necessary, however. You are not our prime suspect. I'm here asking you questions because . . . well, that's my thing: I ask questions. Now, could you pretend for a moment that your thing happens to be *answering* questions? If that's possible, then you can start by answering the question about the paintings. Insured or not insured?"

"Yes," Tuck replied, returning to the desk. "Insured." He settled into his chair again. "But insured for only a portion of their worth," he added.

"Oh?"

"The difference between what the paintings are insured for and what they would have brought at the auction is, conservatively, about a quarter of a million dollars. That will be my actual loss."

34

"Isn't that rather sloppy insuring?" Ironside asked. "It doesn't sound like the work of a man who attends very carefully to details."

"Values in the art market fluctuate a great deal," Tuck replied. "If I had intended to keep the paintings, I would have had them reinsured for a higher figure. But I saw no point in it since I intended to put them up for sale. I didn't anticipate this theft, you see."

"Uh-huh."

"Mr. Tuck —" Eve began.

"Aha!" Tuck broke in, grinning. "I wondered if you were really a policewoman. I thought perhaps you were simply a friend. It was an understandable doubt, was it not? Who would believe that a policewoman could be so attractive? But now you are about to prove me wrong. You're going to ask a policewoman-type question, aren't you?"

"Well . . . yes. . . ." Eve replied, a bit flustered.

He grinned again. "Fire away."

"I was simply wondering why you wanted to sell the paintings."

Tuck pulled at his chin, looking thoughtful. "I'd had my fun out of them, I suppose," he replied finally. "I bought them as an investment, and their value had increased — which is the point of an investment — and I decided the time was right to sell. So, naturally, I sold. Or, rather, I intended to sell. Those drivers —"

"The thieves," Ironside interrupted. "We're not able to prove yet, Mr. Tuck, that Buckley and Jones stole

35

the paintings. So let's refer to the thieves simply as 'the thieves,' shall we?"

Tuck shrugged.

"You mean, then, that you had no interest in the paintings as paintings?" Eve asked.

"They were nice pictures," Tuck answered. "But, as I said, they were primarily an investment." His smile returned. "We all enjoy ourselves in different ways," he said to Eve. "I happen to enjoy the process of making money. It's a form of gambling. Believe me, there are risks."

"But not as many for born winners," Mark put in quickly.

Tuck cocked his head. "There is a man," he said, indicating Mark, "who knows a bit about gambling. He is right. There are born winners and born losers. I happen to be one of the winners."

"Well, this is fascinating conversation," Ironside said, "but it isn't getting the crime solved. I'm sure you're busy. We don't want to take up any more of your time than is absolutely necessary." He was turning his wheelchair toward the doorway. "We'll be talking to each other again, I'm sure."

Mark moved toward the door to open it, and Eve rose and tagged after Ironside.

"I'll go down with you," Tuck said, getting up. "Would you be interested in a tour of the castle and the grounds?"

"Thank you. Some other time," Ironside answered.

36

"I bought it as a setting for the paintings, you know," Tuck said, walking beside Eve.

"I read that," Ironside said, propelling himself through the doorway. "But now I wonder about it. A setting for paintings that were in your words, simply an investment."

Tuck laughed. "It proves how wise it is not to believe everything you read — or hear," he said. "Actually the castle is an investment, too. A man with a castle like this can borrow almost any amount of money he wants. And I operate on borrowed money. I borrow it, invest it elsewhere, and keep the difference between the interest I pay on the loan and the gross profit. If you work with big enough sums, it can be quite profitable. The secret, of course," he said, glancing at Mark, "is to be a born winner."

They had cleared Mrs. Alcorn's small office and entered the corridor.

"I see you still have quite a bit of art on the premises," Ironside said, indicating the paintings on the two walls. "Is that one guard at the gate enough to protect them?"

"A French poodle would be enough to guard these," Tuck replied. "They're very inexpensive. There are a great many of this kind in the castle. I had them mixed in with the valuable things. In fact, there were even quite a few reproductions of the valuable paintings."

"Duplicates?" Eve asked.

"Copies," Tuck answered. "That way, if a thief did break in, he'd have to be an expert to know the authentic

37

paintings from the fake paintings."

"Is that the only protection they had?" Ironside asked.

"No. The usual — alarm system and so forth. And when the valuable paintings were hanging here, I had more guards."

They reached the elevator. The car was waiting, with the door open. Ironside wheeled his chair into it, followed by Eve, then Mark, then Tuck.

"We can find our way out, Mr. Tuck," Ironside said.

"That's all right. I'm not that rushed at the moment." He pressed the button, the door slid closed, and the car began the descent. "You have living quarters directly above the police station, I understand," he said to Ironside. "That must be interesting. Poker — that's your game, isn't it?"

Ironside glanced at him speculatively. "Poker, yes, and pool."

"Eight ball, I'll bet."

Ironside nodded.

"How did you know that?" Eve asked Tuck.

"I'm not always busy with business." He grinned. "I read the newspapers occasionally, and, naturally, I've seen pieces on the Chief."

"And remembered the details quite well," Eve commented.

"I have that kind of mind," Tuck said.

When the car reached the main floor and the door opened, Ironside was the first out. He led the way toward

38

the exit. He seemed to be hurrying. Puzzled, Eve glanced at Mark, and, in reply, he shrugged.

"For any additional questions you might have, I'm at your service," Tuck said to Ironside, halting as Mark pulled open the main door. "I have offices in the city, too, so if it were ever necessary for me to come to headquarters it would be no inconvenience."

"Good," Ironside said noncommittally.

Tuck saluted casually, then turned and walked in the direction from which they had come.

"Let's get out of here," Ironside said gruffly to Mark.

A few minutes later, when they reached the parkway and were on their way back to the city, Ironside said to Eve, "What was his object?"

"Intellectual curiosity," she replied.

Ironside snorted.

"I mean it," Eve insisted. "There for a second I thought he was going to get down on his knees and beg you to invite him to one of your Saturday night poker parties."

"*That* is intellectual curiosity?"

"Yes. He realizes how much alike you and he are. He'd like to observe you. He thinks he could learn a lot about himself, and he probably could. Have you learned anything about yourself by studying him?"

Ironside looked at her blankly. "Pardon?"

"You told me yourself that when you see anything written about him, you read it. And he reads about you, too. It's a mutual fascination. Because, under the tough hide, you two realize how much alike you are."

"I'm as poor as the proverbial church mouse," Ironside pointed out.

"Only because you chose police work instead of making money. Wouldn't you say, though, that you're a success — a major success — at your work?"

"I'm probably not the biggest failure in the trade," Ironside admitted.

"And how did you get to be a success? First, I guess, because you're a natural. And second, because you devote every waking moment to your work — thinking about all those details."

Ironside grunted.

"Admit it. Am I right?"

"Not entirely," he replied. "The moment he introduced himself, he said, 'call me Dave,' or something like that. Do I go around inviting people to 'call me Bob' five seconds after I meet them?"

"No. I'm sure there are little differences. Basically, though, I'm sure you're the same. You're tough. You both had to be to get where you are. And you —"

"Have hearts of gold," Ironside broke in. "All right, all right, perhaps we do have some similarities. The fact of whether we do or don't is irrelevant, though. We're supposed to be on a case. And Tuck, to one degree or another, is a suspect. So what did you think?"

"He had absolutely nothing to do with it," Eve replied. "Why would he want to steal his own paintings? Even though they were insured, he's still losing a quarter

40

of a million dollars. I don't understand."

"So he says, at least."

"Meaning what?"

Ironside wheeled himself to the phone and dialed a number. A few moments later he had Gerard Mehl, the owner of the auction house, on the phone. He told Mehl Tuck's estimate of the difference between the amount of the insurance and the amount the paintings would be likely to bring at the sale. Mehl agreed that it was a reasonable estimate.

When he hung up, Ironside said to Eve, "Of course, we'll have to check to make sure that's how much they were insured for."

"Do you doubt it?"

"No," he replied. "That would be a stupid thing to lie about. Check on it, anyway."

"Right."

Turning his head, Ironside called to Mark. "Have you been listening? What's your opinion of Tuck?"

"I'll tell you one way he's not like you," Mark replied. "He depends on being a born winner. You don't do that. Or do you?"

"I don't think I do," Ironside replied.

"It's a lot like depending on luck," Mark continued. "And you know how luck can let you down. It can build you up, and then, when you need it most, it can be out of town."

"Maybe he was just being modest, calling himself a born winner, intimating that he's just been lucky," Iron-

41

side said. "I don't suppose it's impossible."

"Maybe," Mark replied, without conviction.

"This is a complete waste," Eve said. "We already know that Tuck couldn't have been involved. He had no motive. I know he's very, very rich and he can probably deduct the loss, but isn't that a lot of trouble to go to just to reduce your income?"

Ironside spoke to Mark again. "Shall I tell her, or do you want to?"

"You tell her," Mark replied. "I'm driving."

"Tell me what?" Eve asked in bewilderment.

"Just suppose —" Ironside replied — "just suppose that Tuck did steal those paintings. What would he have right now?"

"Nothing. He'd have the insurance money and he'd have — Oh, I see. Not only would he have the insurance money, but he'd also have the paintings, wouldn't he?" She shook her head. "An ordinary thief, yes, might do that. But a man who lives in a castle like that?"

"Apparently you weren't listening when Tuck told us he lives in that castle for business reasons," Ironside replied. "Translated, I suspect that means, number one, that he doesn't own the castle but simply leases it from the heirs, and, number two, that Mr. Tuck may not be as financially secure as he would appear to be."

"Stealing those paintings, though. . . ." Eve shook her head doubtfully.

"It seems unlikely, doesn't it?" Ironside agreed. "Here's a man with a financial interest in a great

42

number of companies, and a reputation as a sort of middle-aged boy wonder when it comes to making money out of money. Would a man like that involve himself in something as small-time as —" He stopped, then, shaking his head, finished. "But it isn't small-time. It's a matter of several million dollars."

"Only a fraction of what he's worth, though, I'll bet," Eve said.

"You're right," Ironside agreed. "We'd be wasting our time trying to chase down a connection between the theft and David Tuck. It's preposterous."

"Which gets us right back to where we started," Eve said. "Our most likely suspects are Mr. Buckley and Mr. Jones."

"And Mr. Mehl," Ironside reminded her. "I had the feeling that both he and Buckley were holding out on us. I could almost smell a conspiracy."

Mark spoke up again. "I got a whiff of a bad odor myself," he said. "It was back there at that castle."

"Mark," Ironside said gruffly, "Tuck has too much going for him to get himself mixed up in a messy deal like this. Look at it logically. Does a man with his reputation and obvious ability go a route like that?"

"It's happened," Mark replied. "It happens when a man like that, who depends on luck, looks around and finds his luck is out of town. He panics."

Ironside took in a deep breath, then exhaled slowly, looking slightly disturbed. "I'll keep that in mind," he said.

3 Smoke Screen

DET. SGT. ED BROWN looked tired. His shoulders were slumped, his tie was loose and dangling like a hangman's rope, and his jacket was slung over his back, hooked on a curled finger.

Ironside, seated near a window in his living quarters that overlooked the street below, watched Ed Brown cross the large main room and drop into a chair.

"You work too fast; that's why you're exhausted," Ironside said. "I assume that you wouldn't be here if you hadn't finished checking on all of Gerard Mehl's

44

hired help; and if you've finished checking on all those employees, you're working too fast. You must have missed something."

At that moment Mark appeared from the kitchen, carrying a mug of coffee for Ironside. Seeing Ed and his condition of weariness, he said, "How come you're up so early? Aren't you used to sleeping till noon?"

Ed finally stirred himself to respond. "The next time I have information for anybody at this address," he said, "I plan to phone it in. After working straight through the night, a man does not particularly appreciate sadistic humor."

Mark started to hand the coffee to Ironside, then changed his mind. "The patient needs it more than you do, doctor," he said. He took the mug of coffee to Ed, put it in his hand, and headed back to the kitchen to get another for his boss.

"I hope you came up with something worthwhile after working all night and then coming in here and flimflamming my coffee from my chef," Ironside said.

"A couple things," Ed replied, sitting up and sipping the coffee. "For one, Frank Buckley has a record," he said, leaning forward. "He fell once for breaking and entering and once for actual theft. He served his time, however. Right now he's clean."

"Jones?" Ironside asked.

Ed shook his head. "There's nothing so far on Arnold Jones. But listen to what else I found. This was pure chance. I happened to mention to the desk sergeant

45

that I was working on a case involving David Tuck, and he remembered that there'd been a call to come to the Tuck place last Wednesday. It came from a Mrs. . . . uh. . . ." He put a hand into his jacket pocket to get his notes.

"A Mrs. Alcorn?" Ironside said.

"Right," Ed replied, having found the notepaper on which he had written the name. "How did you know?"

"A guess. She's Tuck's secretary."

Ed nodded. "That's right, you were out there. Okay. Anyway, the call came in. The patrol car in the sector was sent out there, but it was too late. Mrs. Alcorn said the problem was solved and the police were no longer needed. She asked them to forget it. So the entry was made, and that was that. But —"

"Now, what were they called for?" Ironside asked gruffly.

"Tuck, it seems, was having a problem with one of his employees — a Harry Tournabeau. I talked to one of the men who answered the summons to the Tuck place. Luckily he'd asked some questions while he was there. So I —"

"That wasn't luck," Ironside said, breaking in. "That was good police work."

"Right. Anyway —"

"Robert T. Ironside is not a man who depends on luck — or, to put it another way, on being a born winner," Mark said, bringing the mug of coffee.

"Is *anybody* interested in hearing what I have to say,

46

after I worked all night getting it?" Ed asked.

"I'm listening," Ironside assured him. "The man's name is Harry Tournabeau and — And what?"

"He's fairly young, about thirty, probably. And he was Tuck's right-hand man. *Very* close to him. But what Tuck had called us for was to have him tossed off the property. Now, I, for one, find that pretty interesting."

"Indeed it is." Ironside nodded. "Have you checked into it further?"

"There's no record on him," Ed replied. "I put in a call to the Tuck place to find out if all had been forgiven and he was still associated with Tuck. I talked — *very* briefly — to this Mrs. Alcorn and got the general idea that if Tournabeau ever showed up around there again he'd be, at the very least, trespassing."

"All right," Ironside said. "Now —"

He was interrupted by the appearance of Policewoman Eve Whitfield as she approached down the ramp that had been installed to make it easier for Ironside to arrive and depart by wheelchair. Mark got coffee for Eve. Ironside and Eve then told Ed about their visit to the Tuck estate, and Ed advised Eve of what he had found out about Frank Buckley and Harry Tournabeau.

"Every time we turn over another stone, we find something that points to Frank Buckley," Eve said. "Isn't it about time for us to bring him in for a more thorough questioning?"

Ironside did not appear to be particularly enthusiastic about the idea. "What exactly would we ask him?" he

47

said. "We don't really have any new information. Tuck told us pretty much the same as what Buckley and Jones claimed. And we covered that with Buckley. I suppose we could ask him, point-blank, if he did it. But I have very little hope that if he did he'd tell us so just because we asked him."

"But we *do* have something new," Eve argued. "We know now that he has a record."

"Yes." Ironside nodded. He frowned. "I wonder if Gerard Mehl knows it. Wouldn't he check into the background of a man who would be required to handle thousands — millions — of dollars' worth of paintings? And if he knew about Buckley's record, would he hire him?"

"No," Eve said, shaking her head.

"Don't be too sure," Mark said. "People have been known to hire people with records, you know."

"Of course, but I'm talking about this particular situation."

"I still say, don't be too sure."

"Apparently," Ironside said, "if I want to know the answer, I'll have to ask elsewhere, since there seems to be some disagreement on the matter here. Ed," he went on, "get an hour's sleep, then pick up where you left off. I want to know as much as possible about all of Gerard Mehl's employees."

"Thanks for the hour, anyway," Ed groaned, pushing himself up out of the chair.

"Eve, find this Harry Tournabeau," Ironside ordered.

"If he was Tuck's right-hand man, he probably had personal property at the Tuck estate or at one of the other Tuck offices. That may mean that it was sent to him. Get on the phone to Mrs. Alcorn. Tell her simply that we want to talk to Tournabeau. If she's indignant about it, tell her we don't have time for that. If you have to, talk directly to Tuck. He'll understand why we want to get in touch with Tournabeau. Tell him we're being thorough, and Tournabeau is a detail."

"Right." Eve smiled.

Ironside motioned to Mark. "Let's travel," he said. "I want to find out how much Gerard Mehl knows — or will admit he knows — about his trusted employees."

Accompanied by Mark, Ironside arrived at the auction house about a half hour later. Gerard Mehl came out of his office to meet him, evidently hoping in that way to keep Ironside's visit short. Ironside ignored the effort, however, wheeling himself straight past Mehl and into his inner sanctum. Mehl, annoyed, and Mark, amused, tagged along.

"No, don't offer me any coffee," Ironside said to Mehl. "I've already had mine."

"If you'd telephoned me," Mehl began, "I probably could have —"

"And deprive myself of your delightful company?" Ironside smiled. "I'll make this as brief as possible, though," he went on. "I don't want to impose on your hospitality. I have some questions."

"I assumed that." Mehl seated himself at his desk.

49

"Why didn't you tell me that Frank Buckley has a record?"

Mehl looked at Ironside squarely for a second, then lowered his eyes. "What sort of a record?"

"Mr. Mehl . . . please. . . ."

Gerard Mehl sighed, nodding. "Yes, of course, I know about it," he said. "Do you know about my brother-in-law, too?"

Ironside's eyebrows arched. "You have a brother-in-law with a record, too?"

"Obviously you don't know about him," Mehl replied. "My brother-in-law is a parole officer. He recommended Frank Buckley to me. He told me that Frank was a man who wanted to go straight but, because of his limitations, could not get a job. He thought I might be able to find a place for him."

"What limitations?" Ironside asked.

"His record, of course, and the fact that he had no skill. Frank is not the brightest man in the world. *But he is a good worker, and I trust him.*"

"You trust him so much, in fact, that you lied to me about his record."

"I didn't lie to you," Mehl protested.

"You failed to tell me about it, Mr. Mehl," Ironside said. "That is a lie of omission."

Mehl got up and walked to a window and stood with his back to Ironside and Mark. "I was aware of how it looked," he said. "If I were in your shoes, Chief, I'd be pretty sure that Frank stole those paintings. But I didn't believe it — and I still don't believe it. So I saw no reason to add to the evidence against him by mentioning his record."

"In the first place," Ironside said, "a record is not evidence. In the second place, you must have known that, sooner or later, I'd find out about it."

"Yes, I suppose so." Mehl nodded, his back still to Ironside. "I just didn't want to be the one to tell you about it, that's all. I have complete trust in Frank."

"I wonder why Frank Buckley didn't mention it," Ironside said.

"For the same reason. He knew the situation looked bad for him and that mentioning his past mistakes would make it look even worse."

"But not as bad as it looks now — for the reason that he withheld the information," Ironside said. "I'd like to talk to him again. Would you ask him to come in here, please?"

Gerard Mehl turned from the window to face Ironside. "I can't do that," he said. "He isn't here. I gave Frank — and Arnold Jones, too — a few days off. I didn't particularly need them. And I thought that, after the unpleasantness, they would benefit by getting away for a day or so."

"Then I'll go to his home," Ironside said. "I assume that you have his address."

Mehl nodded. He returned to his desk. Using the intercom, he asked his secretary to give Frank Buckley's address to Ironside.

"It's one of those residence hotels, I believe," Mehl told Ironside. "He isn't married, and he lives alone, as far as I know."

When Ironside and Mark left Mehl's office, the secretary handed Ironside a slip of paper on which she had noted Frank Buckley's address. Upon reaching the van, Ironside put in a call to Det. Sgt. Ed Brown. He asked that they meet outside Buckley's hotel.

Ed was waiting in his car when the converted paddy wagon pulled up in front of the hotel in a lower-class section of the city. He got out when he saw the van arrive, then joined Ironside, climbing up into the front seat beside Mark.

"For your information," Ed said, "it wasn't an hour."

"What wasn't?"

"That hour of sleep I was supposed to get."

Ironside waved aside the complaint. "This may be something," he said. "Mehl and Buckley deliberately tried to hide the fact that Buckley has a record." He indicated the hotel. "This is where Buckley lives. He should be here. I want you to ask him to come out here so I can talk to him."

"Couldn't Mark have done that?" Ed asked wearily.

"No," Ironside replied, "because if Buckley objects to talking to me here, then I want you to take him in. That Mark couldn't do."

Ed nodded. "Okay."

Ed climbed down and entered the hotel. He was gone almost a quarter of an hour. Then he returned alone.

52

"No Buckley," Ed reported. "The guy at the desk told me he left this morning — he thinks — and he hasn't seen him since. He gave me the key, and I went to Buckley's room and looked. It seems to be in order; the clothes are still there. But, of course, that doesn't mean he hasn't skipped. He could be traveling light."

"Go back in and tell the clerk to give me a call if and when Buckley comes back," Ironside ordered.

When Ed returned, Ironside told him to lock his car and join him in the van. "I'm taking you for a ride."

A few minutes later, with Mark at the wheel and Ironside and Ed Brown in back, the van pulled away from the curb and out into traffic.

"To the Tuck estate," Ironside said to Mark. "Just to the gate, though, this time. Then turn around and drive to the auction house. I want to check the route and the timing."

"What about Buckley?" Ed asked. "Aren't we going to do anything about him? You were certainly anxious a while ago to get hold of him — when you got me up after a half-hour sleep."

"Are you going to hold a grudge about that sleep?" Ironside asked.

In reply, Ed yawned.

"I'll assume that was an apology," Ironside said.

"Apology? Apology for what?"

"For being picayunish about a thing that's as unimportant as sleep. To answer your question, I'm not going to do anything about Buckley at the moment. I have

53

no reason to believe that he's skipping out on us. Besides, with a man like Frank Buckley, the longer he waits — knowing he's wanted — the more nervous he gets. And the more nervous he gets, the more talking he does when he finally starts to talk."

"Do you really think you have something on him?" Ed asked.

Ironside shrugged. "Who knows?"

"Do you really think he's smart enough to have worked this out on his own?" Ed asked.

"No," Ironside replied. "I'm not really after Buckley. I wouldn't be surprised to find out that Buckley did the actual work — the actual lifting of the paintings. But he isn't the one who planned the job."

"Gerard Mehl?" Mark suggested from the front seat.

"Let's think about it," Ironside said. He addressed Ed Brown. "Mehl went out of his way today to pass himself off as 'all heart.' He has a brother-in-law, he told us, who's a parole officer. The brother-in-law sent Frank Buckley to him, and Mehl befriended him by putting him to work."

"So?" Ed asked. "That seems like a pretty nice thing to do."

"Yes, if it happened that way," Ironside replied. "But suppose that, in fact, it happened this way: Gerard Mehl said to his brother-in-law, 'When you find a big, dumb con you think I can manipulate, send him over.' That would put a different connotation on it, wouldn't it?"

Ed nodded.

54

"It's just possible that Gerard Mehl is the one who figured this out, and that he needed a patsy," Ironside continued. "Wouldn't you say, offhand, that Frank Buckley might make a fairly handy patsy?"

"Well. . . ."

"I'm only talking in possibilities," Ironside reminded him.

"Still. . . ."

"If you'd been with us when we were with Gerard Mehl a few hours ago, I think you'd be more inclined to agree," Ironside said. "I got the impression that he was acting. I'm not convinced that he's that bighearted. Why didn't he mention Buckley's record to us? He *knew* we'd find out about it. Maybe it was part of the act, part of trying to make us believe that he only wanted to protect Buckley from us." He shook his head. "It didn't play."

"You're a cynic." Ed grinned.

"I hope not. I try to be a realist, though."

"Then why aren't we chasing after Buckley?"

"Because maybe we got a break not finding him right away," Ironside replied. "If he did the dirty work for Mehl, and Mehl has something on him, the longer Buckley sweats it out — that is, sweats out the fact that we're looking for him — the softer he'll be when we catch him. Am I right?"

"Theoretically."

"Then let's just let it ride and let Buckley soften," Ironside said.

"You know," Mark said from the front seat, "if you follow that theory all the way to the end, the best way to catch a criminal would be to let him go."

Ironside chuckled appreciatively.

When they reached the narrow road that led to the Tuck estate, Ironside had Mark stop the van.

"How far, in time, is it from the castle to here?" he asked.

"Oh . . . a few minutes," Mark replied.

"Good. Now let's drive straight from here to the auction house. Not fast, not slow. Keep to the speed limit. Pretend that you're delivering several million dollars' worth of paintings. Then when we get there we'll add three minutes."

Not much was said on the way back toward the city. The three paid particular attention to the turnoffs along the parkway, looking for one that might give thieves some special opportunity to exchange the crates carried by two trucks. But they saw nothing that suggested an obvious location.

"There just wasn't enough camouflage," Ironside said as the van entered the city. "They'd be taking too big a chance, pulling that truck off the parkway, shifting the crated paintings to a different truck, and replacing them with fifty-seven empty crates from the other truck. It was broad daylight. How could a scene like that be missed?"

"It'd be a lot different here in the city, though, wouldn't it?" Mark said. "If they just had the right connections, couldn't they pull into one of these parking garages?"

"A very distinct possibility," Ironside replied, "but which parking garage?" He turned to Ed. "When you pick up where you left off in checking on Buckley and Jones and Mehl," he said, "look for something like that — a connection with a parking garage or some privately owned building along this route. A relative might own one . . . or a friend . . . or an associate. You know what I mean."

"Got it." Ed nodded.

A few minutes later they arrived at the auction house. "Very, very close," Ironside said, looking at his watch. "Only a couple minutes' difference between our time and Frank Buckley's on the day he brought the paintings in."

"The day he brought the empty crates in," Ed corrected him.

"Yes."

"But can we rely on Buckley's estimate of how long it took?" Mark asked.

"It correlates very well with what both David Tuck and Gerard Mehl told us," Ironside replied. "Now, one of those men might be lying, of course. Mehl, in particular, might be. But at the moment it's all we have to go on."

"One or all of them have to be lying," Ed said. "Paintings just don't disappear into thin air. And we know that if Buckley didn't stop, then there wasn't time

57

to shift crates from one vehicle to another."

Ironside nodded. "You're right; two men couldn't have accomplished it that fast," he said. "A crew, perhaps, could have done it. But this is not that kind of job. There's no sign of any professionals being mixed up in it."

"Buckley has a record," Mark reminded him. "He could have ties with the pros."

"Possible," Ironside agreed. He was not particularly taken with the idea, however. "Let's go back to Headquarters," he said. "Maybe Eve had found that other fellow. What's his name?"

"Harry Tournabeau," Ed said.

"Yes, him." Ironside nodded.

Mark pulled back out into traffic and headed the paddy wagon toward the police department's central headquarters. In the back, Ironside and Ed Brown sat frowning as they pondered.

A while later Mark made a sudden turn. Surprised, Ironside and Ed Brown had to hold on to keep from being thrown off-balance.

"What was that?" Ironside asked irritably.

"Testing," Mark replied. "I'll tell you in a second."

He made another sharp turn.

"Can't you think of any *nice* games to play?" Ironside complained.

"We've got a tail," Mark replied. "That blue Chevy, four cars back."

Ironside and Ed looked out the rear window.

58

"How long has he been with us?" Ironside asked.

"Since we pulled away from the auction house, for sure," Mark replied. "But now that I know he's tailing us, I have the vague impression that he's been with us all along, maybe ever since we left Buckley's hotel."

"Any suggestions?" Ironside said. "He's playing it pretty smart, hanging back like that."

"There's a dead end up ahead about six blocks," Mark said. "I could pull in there and swing around, and maybe we could trap him."

"It's worth a try, I suppose," Ironside decided.

Mark proceeded at the same speed until he reached the dead-end street. He made the turn, then speeded up, suddenly hit the brakes, whipped around, and drove in the direction from which he had just come.

By then the Chevy had reached the turn and had started into the dead-end street. The driver saw the van headed toward him, however. He quickly braked and put the Chevy into reverse.

"He's going to get away!" Ed shouted.

Mark slammed on the brakes. He jumped from the doorway on the driver's side, and Ed leaped out the rear door at the same time. The two men — Ed with his pistol drawn — raced toward the car that had been following them.

By then the Chevy had backed up about fifty yards, though. As Ed and Mark approached, the car suddenly bucked forward, then, with tires squealing, turned back into the traffic and raced away.

59

"Did you get a look at him?" Ed said to Mark. "Was it who I thought it was?"

"I wouldn't swear to it," Mark replied, "but my guess would be that it was Frank Buckley."

They returned to the van, and Ed told Ironside that both he and Mark were almost positive that Frank Buckley had been behind the wheel of the Chevy.

"Do you suppose he was waiting for us somewhere near his hotel?" Ironside said. "If he was, then Gerard Mehl may have alerted him that we were on our way to talk to him."

"But why follow us if he wanted to stay away from us?" Mark asked.

Ironside shook his head in puzzlement. "This case gets curiouser and curiouser," he said. "It's the kind where the most sensible solution seems to be to put all the suspects in a bag, then shake it up and turn it over. The one that falls out first is the guilty party. I think —"

His phone was ringing.

Ironside picked up the receiver, listened for a few minutes, speaking very little, then hung up. He told Mark to drive them to a hotel in the center of the city.

"Who do we know there?" Ed asked. "That's for the rich folks."

"David Tuck," Mark guessed. "He probably owns the place."

"Wrong," Ironside said. "That was Eve. She's located Harry Tournabeau. He has a suite, and he's there now. We're going calling."

Ed yawned. "I hope he isn't using his bedroom," he said. "While you're interrogating him, maybe I can get a few more winks of sleep."

"Mark!" Ironside called. "Make a detour. We want to drop Ed off."

Ed frowned. "I didn't mean that," he said. "I can sleep anytime. Frankly, I'd rather meet this ex-right-hand man. This case is beginning to get to me. The deeper we get into it, the more confusing it becomes."

Ironside shook his head. "No, Ed. There are other things that are just as important as interrogating witnesses and/or suspects."

"But sleep isn't one of them," Ed protested.

"Who said anything about sleep? I only told Mark to drop you off. I meant to drop you off at Headquarters, so you can pick up where you left off with that investigation of Gerard Mehl and his employees."

Ed sighed deeply. "I have a distinct feeling that I'm losing," he muttered.

4 Cold Reception

IRONSIDE AND MARK dropped Ed off at Headquarters, then proceeded to The Hill, the exclusive hotel from which Eve had telephoned. After parking the van, they entered the lobby. Eve, who had been seated near the entrance, joined them.

"What took you so long?" she asked.

"We had a delivery to make," Mark chuckled.

"Is he still here?" Ironside asked Eve.

"I assume so. The clerk thought so. He has suite seventeen-o-nine." She nodded toward the desk. "I got it from the clerk. Would you like to be announced, or would you prefer just to drop in?"

"Let's announce," Ironside decided. "We're not raiding Mr. Tournabeau. We're paying him a friendly visit."

They moved on to the house phones. Ironside made the call to Harry Tournabeau's suite. Tournabeau was surprised, but he had no objection to answering some questions.

Ironside, Eve, and Mark arrived at Tournabeau's suite a few minutes later. It was large and luxuriously furnished and had a breathtaking view of the bay. It seemed obvious that, having lost his job, Tournabeau had not been forced to go on welfare.

Tournabeau was fairly young, evidently in his late twenties. He had old-looking eyes, however, and a taut, skeptical manner. He was dressed in slacks and loafers and a sport shirt, but even in these casual clothes he managed to look businesslike.

When the introductions were completed, Ironside said, "I suppose you know what brings us here."

Tournabeau shook his head. "No."

"Haven't you read or heard about the paintings?"

"Oh, yes," he replied, "but I had no way of knowing what you're investigating. I know Dave Tuck quite well, you see, so I'm aware of a number of things that you might be looking into."

Ironside raised an eyebrow. "Things about Mr. Tuck that would interest the police? For instance?"

63

Tournabeau forced a tight smile. "I'm not an informer," he replied. "If you have specific questions, I'll give you specific answers. But don't expect me to volunteer information."

Ironside was silent for a second, then he said, "I understand that you and Mr. Tuck parted on the worst of terms."

"Did he tell you that?"

"I'm aware that he called the police to have you ejected from the premises."

"Yes, we had words," Tournabeau replied. "And I'll admit he was justified, as he saw it, in dismissing me. Do you want to know why he did it?"

"I don't know," Ironside replied. "Why don't you tell me? Then I'll be able to decide whether I want to know or not."

"He was doing some maneuvering on the stock market," Tournabeau replied, "hoping to pick up enough stock to move in on a certain company. He was doing it gradually and quietly, but, in spite of that, the price of the stock was advancing rapidly. It was becoming quite costly for him. It seemed that somebody knew what he was trying to do."

"You?" Ironside guessed.

"Yes."

"His right-hand man was taking advantage of inside information and was using it to help himself and hurt Tuck. Is that right?"

"Correct," Tournabeau replied. "The fact is correct,

64

at least," he added. "The interpretation is not, however. You make it sound like a terrible thing. How do you think Dave Tuck got where he is? By playing it smart, that's how."

"Playing it dirty, I think, is the appropriate phrase." Ironside smiled. "But I'm not here to pass judgment. As a matter of fact, now that I know why you and Tuck had your falling out, I would just as soon *not* know." He made a sweeping motion, indicating the surroundings. "May I ask if you have an independent income, Mr. Tournabeau?"

Tournabeau frowned. "I have an income," he replied. "I have investments. But what business is that of yours?"

"Nosiness," Ironside replied. "You're aware, I suppose, of the value of the paintings that were stolen."

"Yes, I —" He leaned forward. "Are you suggesting that *I* stole them? That I'm able to live well because I stole those paintings and peddled them?" He shook his head. "That's preposterous. If that's the lead you're following, you're wasting your time completely."

"I didn't even suggest it," Ironside replied calmly.

Tournabeau got up from his seat and walked to a table near where Eve was sitting. "Tuck is the one you want," he said. He got a cigar from a humidor that was sitting near the center of the table, then headed back toward his chair. "I don't mean to imply that he stole the paintings, but I would guess that he himself arranged for it. He's in trouble, you know."

Ironside and Eve exchanged glances.

"No, I didn't know that," Ironside said.

"The structure of his so-called empire had developed some cracks," Tournabeau said, sitting down again and picking up a lighter from the small table beside the chair. "He needs cash now, not paintings. So he had the paintings lifted, and within a few days he'll have money from the insurance. It's as simple as that."

"You can prove this, I assume," Ironside said.

"Of course not," Tournabeau replied. He touched the flame of the lighter to the tip of the cigar. "But, in his place, it's what I'd do."

"I don't doubt that in the least." Ironside smiled coldly. "There happens to be a hole in your theory, however," he went on. "As I understand it, Tuck could have got more money for the paintings by selling them than by collecting the insurance on them."

"That's what he'd like you to believe, I'm sure," Tournabeau said. "But those paintings were fakes, you know."

Ironside studied him. "Oh?"

"Of course."

For the first time Eve spoke up. "Do you have any proof of *that?*" she asked testily.

Tournabeau glanced at her. "You came here to ask questions," he said. "Why does it make you angry when I answer them?"

"She isn't angry," Ironside said. "She's just, as I am, a bit doubtful. You were only guessing about Tuck being involved in the theft. We deal in proof, Mr. Tournabeau, not speculation. Now, you say you think the paintings are fakes? Why do you think that?"

"I happen to know that Tuck paid an especially high price to have them authenticated," Tournabeau replied. "He wouldn't have done that if it hadn't been necessary, and the need would arise only if the paintings were fakes. It's as simple as that." He knocked the ash off his cigar. "I saw the check that went to Halverson," he said. "He didn't get that kind of money for being honest."

"Halverson?"

"Alver Halverson. He owns the Halverson Gallery. He authenticated the paintings. Halverson has an impeccable reputation for honesty. It costs a great deal to buy a man like that."

"Well, thank you," Ironside said. "We appreciate your willingness to help." He wheeled toward the door. "We might be calling on you again," he said.

"Anything you want to know about Dave Tuck, you come to me," Tournabeau said, rising and following Ironside, Eve, and Mark toward the foyer. "I'm an expert on that subject."

When they had reached the paddy wagon and Ironside and Eve were settled in the back, with Mark again behind the wheel, Mark turned and asked, "Where to now?"

"For the moment, nowhere," Ironside replied. He addressed Eve. "What was your impression?"

"He sounded like a child trying to get somebody in

68

trouble," she replied. "He must be pretty bitter about the break with Mr. Tuck. He made all those accusations, but he had absolutely nothing to back them up."

"It would seem that way," Ironside said. "We can't just discard what he said, though, because to us he seemed a little childish. That notion that Tuck's financial empire is cracking up — that might be pure imagination, sour grapes. But that charge that Tuck paid an extraordinarily high fee to have the paintings evaluated — that interests me. That's the kind of information that Tournabeau, being Tuck's right-hand man, would be likely to have."

"But what is it worth?" Eve asked.

"It could be worth a great deal. Tournabeau is right. Why would Tuck pay more than he had to if the paintings were authentic? The only logical reason I can think of for paying more than necessary is that the paintings *were* fakes and the gallery owner — what was his name? — charged a high fee for evaluating them as genuine."

"Halverson. Alver Halverson."

"That would make Tuck a very hot suspect," Mark said.

"Exactly," Ironside agreed. "He'd have a very good reason for stealing the paintings. Stolen, they'd bring him the insurance money. But put up for auction, they'd probably bring him practically nothing."

"Why?" Eve asked. "They were authenticated."

"But dealers would be at that auction," Ironside explained. "They'd see that the paintings were fakes. The paintings haven't been on display, you know. They've been hanging on Tuck's walls. If the other dealers got a look at them, this whole bit about their value might go right up in smoke."

"Tuck wouldn't look so smart," Mark said.

"I refuse to believe that's how it happened," Eve insisted. "Harry Tournabeau is nothing more than a . . . a. . . ."

"Obviously," Ironside said, "he's not a prime candidate for the 'Honesty Is the Best Policy' award. But we can't ignore his claims just because we don't happen to care much for him personally. I'd like to check further into this idea he has that Tuck's empire — so-called, as Tournabeau would say — is breaking up. If Tuck needs cash and . . . well, anyway, let's see what we can find out."

"Now?" Mark asked.

"Now," Ironside replied. "We'll take Eve to Headquarters."

"What am I going to do at Headquarters?" Eve asked as the van eased out into traffic.

"It'll be your base. Use the phone. Call some of the financial people we know. Get the names of the people Tuck's had dealings with lately. Talk to them. You might pick up a rumor. If you do, track it down. You know the routine."

"You mean you really believe that? That David Tuck is on the skids?"

"It wouldn't be the first time."

70

"For him?"

"No, not for him, but for other multimillionaires. What can be gained can also be lost, you know. They can make mistakes."

"If they pay very close attention to details?"

"Even then."

"Sorry," Eve said. "I just can't picture Mr. Tuck as a loser. He reminds me too much of —" She stopped, started to continue the statement, then changed her mind and became silent.

"I assume you were about to say that he reminds you too much of me," Ironside said.

"Uh-huh."

Ironside closed his hands on the arms of his wheelchair. "And then you recalled that I haven't always been a winner."

Eve did not reply.

"If that's what you thought, it's true," Ironside said. "So remember that when you're checking up on Tuck. A man can look like a sure and constant winner . . . and not be. Do a thorough job. Don't pass up any details."

"Yes, sir."

A few minutes later they reached Headquarters.

"If you need me, I'll be at the Halverson Gallery," Ironside informed Eve. "Oh, yes. If you see Ed, and he seems to be asleep, give him a shake. Tell him there'll be plenty of time to sleep when he goes on vacation, if there's ever time for a vacation."

"I'm sure he'll appreciate that." Eve smiled.

Ironside called up to Mark. "To the Gallery, Picasso!"

It was a half-hour drive through afternoon traffic to Alver Halverson's place of business. It was in a section where most of the city's art galleries were located. When Ironside and Mark entered, it appeared to be deserted, but a few seconds later a young man, neatly and fashionably dressed, appeared from the rear and moved quickly toward them.

"Mr. Halverson?" Ironside said doubtfully.

"Yes?"

"I expected someone a little older. How did you get to be an expert so quickly?"

"I think you're looking for my father." The young man smiled. "Was there something. . . ."

Ironside handed him a card. "I'll need only a few minutes of his time, if he's available," he said.

"I'm sure he will be," the young man replied. He then turned and retreated to the rear of the gallery.

Ironside and Mark looked around. On the walls of the gallery were hung a number of paintings, but they were not crowded.

"Recognize anything?" Ironside asked.

"I could authenticate the walls — genuine plaster," Mark replied.

A moment later a man in late middle age approached them. He was small and rather dumpy, with a kindly, smiling face.

"Chief Ironside, it's an honor," the man said. "My

son told me, but I was doubtful. I recognize you from your pictures, though."

"Mr. Halverson? *Alver* Halverson?"

"Yes. . . ."

"I'm working on a case involving the theft of a number of paintings owned by Mr. David Tuck," Ironside said. "I suppose you read about it in the papers."

Halverson's manner underwent an immediate change. The smile, which had seemed permanent, was gone. He locked his fingers together in front of him and took a sturdy, flat-footed stance, as if to announce that under no circumstances would he be moved from his present position.

"Well, I see you know about the theft," Ironside said. "Was there something about it that particularly disturbed you?"

"No," Halverson replied coldly. "I have no interest in it whatsoever. And I know nothing about it. So if you were expecting to learn something from me, you will be disappointed. I repeat: I know absolutely nothing about it."

"I didn't come here to accuse you of stealing the paintings, Mr. Halverson."

"I can only tell you that I know nothing about it."

Ironside nodded. "You do know something about the paintings, however," he said. "You could hardly have authenticated them without knowing something about them, could you? *That's* what I came here to talk to you about. It has been suggested that perhaps they weren't genuine. I wonder if you would have any comment on that."

"Chief Ironside, as you said, I authenticated the paintings," Halverson replied belligerently. "And since I pronounced them genuine, there can be no doubt at all about the matter."

"Mmmmm, yes . . . well, that's very reassuring. You're positive, absolutely positive, that you couldn't have been wrong?"

"There is no possible chance."

"Other dealers have been wrong about things like that. Haven't I heard about paintings being authenticated by reliable dealers and then later being found to be fakes?"

"It has happened, yes," Halverson replied crisply. "But it has never happened to me."

"Well, there's always a first —"

"Never!" Halverson broke in. "Does that answer your question, Chief Ironside?"

"One of my questions," Ironside replied. "I have another. It concerns the fee that David Tuck paid you when you authenticated the paintings. I'm told —"

Halverson interrupted again. "The fees I charge are my private business," he said. "I do not discuss them with anyone except my clients."

"I'm not particularly interested in dollars and cents. That's between you and the Internal Revenue Service," Ironside said. "I would like to know, though, if it was higher than the fee you usually charge."

"I have nothing to say about that."

"Well, let's assume that —"

"I have given you permission to assume nothing, sir," Halverson snapped.

"Would you say, then, that it was the *same* as the fees you usually charge?"

"Chief Ironside, do not insult me by trying to be clever."

"Sorry." Ironside smiled wryly.

"If that is all. . . ."

"Since I can't seem to hit on anything that you care to discuss, that does rather limit the conversation," Ironside said.

Alver Halverson turned and marched back toward the rear of the gallery. A moment later he had disappeared from sight.

Ironside looked up at Mark. "Do you ever get the impression that we're not universally loved and admired?" he asked.

"Sometimes," Mark replied, "but not this time. He admires you, all right enough. He's just determined not to say the first word about those paintings — and he's a pretty determined man."

Ironside turned his chair and wheeled toward the exit. "As honest as he is determined, would you say?"

"No comment."

"My guess is that he really soaked Tuck for that evaluation and authentication. If he didn't, why wouldn't he talk about it?"

75

Mark opened the door, and Ironside wheeled his way through the opening.

"No comment again," Mark said, letting the door close behind them.

"Why, all of a sudden, these 'no comments'?"

"Because Halverson is a character," Mark replied. "Characters are hard to figure. The minute you convince yourself that they're this way or that way, they turn out to be the other way. I don't know. Maybe Halverson, as you said, soaked Tuck for the evaluation, and maybe he didn't. If he did, maybe it was because the paintings were fakes and he was charging him for a pass, or maybe it wasn't. I'll play it safe and stick with 'no comment.' "

They had reached the paddy wagon. Mark lowered the lift, Ironside wheeled the chair onto it, then Mark raised the platform. When Ironside was inside, Mark closed the door, then took his place at the wheel.

"Home?" Mark asked.

Ironside was deep in contemplation.

"Yeah-hoo! Home?"

"What? Oh . . . yes . . . home. . . ."

Ironside was silent and thoughtful throughout the trip to Headquarters. When they reached their living quarters, Mark went to the kitchen to prepare the lunch they had missed. Ironside stopped his chair in the middle of the large main room and, oblivious to the surroundings, continued to ponder.

A few minutes later Ed Brown came in. "Nothing

more," he reported to Ironside, dropping into a chair. "Gerard Mehl and all of his employees — except Buckley, of course — are completely clean."

Ironside grunted vaguely.

"Did you hear me?"

"What? Oh, yes. Mehl and his people are clean."

"I suppose that eliminates them."

"Nope. The only thing it means is that they don't have a record — not with us, anyway. Nobody ever has a record before he takes that first fall, you know. And you can quote me on that."

"Thanks," Ed chuckled. "What did you find out from Harry Tournabeau?"

Ironside told Ed about the visit to Tournabeau, about sending Eve back to Headquarters to begin a check on Tuck, then about the visit to the Halverson Gallery.

"Busy, busy," Ed commented. "But what's been accomplished? That's what I was saying before about this case. The deeper into it we get, the more confusing it gets. According to the manual, that's not the way it's supposed to be, is it?"

"I don't remember. I haven't looked at the manual in years."

"Theoretically," Ed insisted, "the more information you collect, the closer you get to a solution. What's going wrong?"

"Wrong information, maybe," Ironside said.

Mark arrived with lunch.

"Eat fast," Ironside said to him. "You have some

work to do, and it'll take time."

"Eat fast?" Mark protested, sitting down to the table. "I'm a growing boy. I'm supposed to eat relaxed and chew my food thoroughly, every bite. What work? Where am I going?"

"For a walk," Ironside replied, starting to eat. "Maybe a long walk, maybe a short walk. I want you to take —" He reached into his jacket pocket and got a slip of notepaper. "Buckley gave me this," he said, handing it to Mark. "It's his route, according to him. I want you to take it and follow it —"

"We did that already."

"Will you listen? I want you to follow it and stop in at all the parking garages along the way. Don't go to the head man. Ask around among the attendants. Ask about the truck Buckley was driving. Find out if anybody saw it pull in anywhere. Got it?"

Mark nodded. "It's a wild chance," he said.

"We're not doing too well sticking to the sure things." He turned to Ed Brown. "You can go with him —" he began.

Ed had dropped off to sleep in the chair.

"You almost had an assistant," Ironside said to Mark. "But I guess he wouldn't have been much help to you, anyway. You'd have had to keep shaking him awake to keep him moving."

Mark left about a quarter of an hour later. When he had gone, Ironside called downstairs and asked if Eve were anywhere around. She had been seen earlier, but at the moment she was nowhere in sight. Ironside then made another call, this one to the commissioner.

After exchanging greetings, Ironside got right to the point. "You mix in that arty crowd, don't you? Who can I talk to to get a line on a gallery owner?"

"Which one?" the commissioner asked.

"Alver Halverson." Ironside replied. "Know him?"

"As a matter of fact, I do, Bob. He's a charming old guy. Are you thinking about doing some buying? Halverson's the man you want to talk to. He's the expert's expert, and as honest as the day is long."

"If you don't mind, I think I'll get an opinion from someone else. I just saw Halverson an hour or so ago, and to me he was not a 'charming old guy.' I'd like to talk to some of his competitors and maybe some of the people who've bought from him. Can you give me some names?"

"Yes, sure." The commissioner sounded puzzled. "But what for? I can vouch for Halverson. I told you: He's as honest as the day is long."

"The days are getting shorter," Ironside said with a short laugh. "Now, if you could just give me some names. . . ."

The names were forthcoming, and Ironside spent the next hour and a half making calls. He talked to other gallery owners and to art collectors who regularly dealt with Alver Halverson. Without exception, they had high regard for the man. Gallery owner after gallery owner

79

insisted that if Halverson had authenticated the Tuck paintings, without a doubt they were genuine.

Ironside was slumping, looking disgusted, when Eve appeared a few minutes after he finished making the calls.

She nodded toward Ed, who was still asleep. "Typical alert young police officer?"

"Don't be cute. What did you find out?"

Eve frowned. "Who bit you?"

"I had a nice pat theory, and I checked it out and found it full of holes," he replied. "That kind of thing can destroy a man's faith in himself. Now, I repeat, what did you find out?"

Eve sat down. "Well, nothing exactly, so far. But, to my surprise, I may be on to something. I started in the newspaper morgue. I found a lot of stories on Tuck in the financial pages, of course. So I noted the names of men he'd had any business dealings with, and I began contacting them." She stopped a moment, then went on. "What surprised me was that they weren't surprised," she said. "Not one of them flatly denied the possibility that Tuck might be in financial trouble."

"I'm a little surprised myself," Ironside said.

"A few minutes ago I got a tip," Eve continued. "One of the men suggested that I contact a reporter on the *Journal*. I called him. Roger McCandlish. Do you know him?"

Ironside shook his head. "I know only the reporters on the police beat. What about him?"

80

"I called him and told him I was interested in Tuck and —" She looked at her watch. "I have an appointment with him at the *Journal* office in a half hour."

"Let's just hope he has something we can use," Ironside said. "If he's anything like the reporters I know, all he's interested in is finding out if the nice young police lady is as attractive in person as she sounds over the phone."

"He's not a police reporter. He's a financial writer."

"He's a male, isn't he?"

"Well . . . yes. . . ."

"Good luck — however it turns out," Ironside said.

5 One-Upmanship

AT THE SOUND of Ed Brown stretching and awakening, Ironside maneuvered his wheelchair away from the window and toward Ed's chair.

"Tell me," Ironside said, "are the police supposed to stake out a criminal, or does the criminal stake out the police?"

Ed groaned groggily. "Riddles? At this time of the morning?"

"It isn't morning. You didn't sleep quite that long. It's early evening. I haven't even had dinner yet."

Ed sat up. "Where's Mark?"

"Calling on parking garage attendants. Are you going to answer my question, or must I remain forever ignorant? Do the police tail the criminal, or does the criminal tail the police?"

Ed squinted at him. "What is that supposed to mean?"

Ironside motioned with his head. "Take a look out the window. That fellow who's standing across the street. To me he looks somewhat familiar. That Chevy parked three cars up looks somewhat familiar, too."

Ed rose and went to the window. He stood there for several minutes, then said, "I'm not sure. It looks a lot like Buckley — and that might be his Chevy. But I'm not positive."

"There's a way to find out," Ironside said.

Ed moved toward the door. "If it's Buckley, how do you want him? As a prisoner or as a guest?"

"Let's just be sociable, since we really don't have anything we can charge him with."

When Ed had gone, Ironside wheeled himself back to the window. A few moments later he saw Ed cross the street, then stop and address the man who, from above, looked like Frank Buckley. In replying, the man gestured a great deal with his hands. After another few moments, Ed and the man walked together toward the entrance to Headquarters.

Ironside had been right, he discovered shortly. The man Ed Brown escorted into his quarters was definitely Frank Buckley.

"Welcome!" Ironside smiled. "I was beginning to think we wouldn't ever meet again, Frank. I suppose it was all in my imagination, but I was getting the idea that you were going out of your way to avoid me."

"I don't know what you're talking about," Buckley replied sourly.

Ed spoke up. "He wouldn't say why he was standing across the street," he said.

"He was probably lost," Ironside guessed, "and he was debating whether or not to cross the street and ask a nice policeman to find his hotel for him. Right, Frank?"

"I got enough rights to stand around anywhere I want," Buckley said. "I got a job, Chief. I'm a responsible citizen. You can't pick me up for vagrancy."

"Believe me, that's the farthest thing from my mind," Ironside said. "I wouldn't want to be the one to add to your record, Frank."

Buckley looked down and away. "You dug that up, eh?"

"You knew we would."

"Yeah."

Ironside indicated a chair. "Rest your feet," he said. "How long have you been standing over there?"

Buckley sat down, but he did not reply to the question.

"Or you can use the phone if you'd like to report in to Gerard Mehl," Ironside said.

Buckley's eyes narrowed. "What for?" he asked.

"He's your boss, isn't he?"

"I got a couple days off."

"I wasn't thinking so much about your regular work," Ironside said. "I thought he might want to know that you're still keeping an eye on me — only from a much closer range now."

"What's he got to do with that?" Buckley asked.

"Frank, it's pretty obvious that this all ties in with the paintings. Why did Mehl give you a job at his auction house? It was because he needed somebody with your experience — right?"

"What experience? I couldn't do nothing. He give me a job because I figured I'd try it straight and see if it worked, and he's a guy that'll do something for another guy."

"You had a record, Frank. That implies some experience of a certain kind, doesn't it?"

"Mr. Mehl just wanted to help me, that's all. He's a nice guy. His brother-in-law, he's the guy that sent me to him." He pushed his fingers through his hair, showing nervousness. "He's a parole officer. You can ask him."

Ed entered the conversation again. "Where are the paintings now, Frank?" he asked casually.

"You got it wrong," Buckley replied angrily.

"Why did Mehl warn you that we were on our way to your hotel this morning to talk to you?" Ironside asked.

"He didn't. He didn't tell me nothing."

"But you managed to disappear. What did you do, park across the street from the entrance? Were you watching us when Ed went into the hotel to get you?"

Buckley shook his head. "You're talking a lot of crazy stuff. I don't even know what it is."

"Then you followed us out to the Tuck estate," Ed suggested. "You followed us out, and you followed us back. Why, Frank?"

Buckley wiped perspiration from his upper lip. "Boy, this is wild. You guys are dreaming or something."

"Who ordered you to keep an eye on us?" Ironside asked. "If it wasn't Gerard Mehl, who was it?"

Buckley shook his head. "You're way off . . . way off . . . I don't even know what you're talking about."

"That wasn't you, then, in that Chevy?" Ed asked. "It's just coincidence, I suppose, that the same car is parked across the street right now."

"Look, I own a car, it's a Chevy, and I drive around," Buckley said. "That's what a car's for, right? When you got a car, you drive around."

"You drive into dead ends?"

"You're dreaming again."

"You didn't leave that note in the front seat of my van, either, did you?" Ironside said.

"Note? What note?"

"It was a warning. Perhaps it even could have been interpreted as a threat."

"I don't never threaten nobody," Buckley replied.

"Somebody else left it?" Ironside asked.

"I don't know nothing about it."

"It was your printing, Frank. I compared it with the

86

printing you did when you wrote out the route from the Tuck estate to the auction house for me."

Buckley looked away again.

"There's no doubt about it," Ironside said. "You wrote the note that was left in the van. You tracked us from your hotel to the Tuck estate and then back into the city. Were you following orders from Gerard Mehl?"

Buckley sighed deeply, then shook his head. "He don't know nothing about it," he replied. "I done it on my own."

"Where are the paintings?"

Buckley raised his head and looked squarely at Ironside. "You got it wrong. I been tailing you. But I don't know any more about where them paintings are than nobody."

"Come on, Frank, get it over with," Ed urged. "Where are the paintings?"

Buckley kept his eyes on Ironside. "I don't know nothing about it. That's why I wrote that note. I know enough about you, Chief, that if somebody tells you not to do it, you're going to do it, right?"

Ironside glanced at Ed, then looked back at Buckley. "What is that supposed to mean?"

"He means you're pigheaded," Ed said.

"I asked *him!*" Ironside snapped.

"That's what I meant," Buckley agreed. "I figured if somebody told you to get off the case, you'd stay on it, and nobody'd talk you out of it. So I wrote that note."

"To keep me on the case?" Ironside asked puzzledly.

"It was my best bet," Buckley replied. "I ain't so dumb I can't see how it looks. Here I am with a couple million bucks' worth of goods, and all of a sudden, right out of the blue, it disappears. How does that make me look? I'm a guy with a record. So the only thing I got going for me is the cop on the case."

Ironside exchanged looks with Ed again.

"That's how I figured it," Buckley said.

"I must be missing something," Ironside replied. "Your explanation doesn't make any sense to me."

"It's like this," Buckley said. "No offense, Chief, but there's cops and there's cops. Know what I mean? I mean, cops is just like people, right? Some of them do the best kind of job they can do, and some of them, maybe, bug off a little — right? So, from what I could see, it looked to me like I had my head on the chopping block, and I wanted the right kind of cop on the case before the ax come down. Now you get it?"

"You mean you were sure the Chief would clear you?" Ed asked.

"A hundred percent positive."

"How could you be that sure?" Ironside asked.

"Because I didn't do it," Buckley answered.

"That —"

Ironside was interrupted by the ringing of the phone. He reached out and picked up the receiver and identified himself.

"I may have something," the voice on the other end said, a trifle excitedly. It was Mark calling.

"Pay dirt *already?*" the Chief replied, his tone dubious.

"Yes and no. No, I haven't found anybody who saw the truck pull in, but, yes, I have turned up something that may interest you. It seems that I'm not the only one who's making the rounds of the parking garages, asking questions. Another guy is doing the same thing. And what's even more fascinating is the fact that we're asking the same question."

The Chief was immediately interested. "Fascinating. Has he left his card?"

"No," Mark replied, "but he's left his description behind. Want to play Guess Who?"

There was silence from Ironside.

"I should have known you wouldn't. Anyway, from what I'm told, he looks remarkably like Tournabeau."

"Now, that *is* interesting. I had him penciled in as an innocent bystander. Why would —" Ironside stopped, suddenly realizing that Buckley was listening to his half of the conversation. "I'm getting hungry," he told Mark. "Why don't you break off your little project until tomorrow?"

"I'm on my way," Mark replied, understanding exactly what the Chief meant.

Ironside hung up, then faced Buckley again. "I don't buy your story," he said. "In the first place, it sounds like something out of fantasyland. You're a big boy, Frank — big enough to have tumbled twice. Big boys don't go around playing kiddie games."

"Look, Chief," Buckley replied, "I told it to you like

89

it is. This job I got with Mr. Mehl, it's my last chance — see? I'm no kid no more. I can't learn no trade. But I can push a broom and drive a truck and wrestle crates around. So this job I got, it's more than just a job, like it'd be to some guys — like to Jones, for instance. See what I mean? If I lose it, where do I go?"

Ironside looked at him hard.

"I'll tell you the place I don't want to go," Buckley went on. "It's back to the jug. I been there, and I don't like it. You know? If I fall again, when they put me in they'll throw away the key, right? I don't want that. And the way I see it, the best insurance I got is you."

Ironside turned the wheelchair and wheeled toward the window.

"You can call it kid stuff if you want," Buckley went on. "Maybe it was. But I was pretty desperate. It looked bad for me, right? So, I wrote that note. I wanted you on the case."

Ironside had reached the window. "When did I say I might not stay on the case?"

"You didn't say nothing. I just didn't want to take no chances."

"You wrote the note, then you started tailing me?"

"I wanted to make sure," Buckley replied. "I figured I could tell by where you came and went whether you were sticking on the case or not. I couldn't call you up and ask you, could I?"

"Okay," Ironside said gruffly.

90

"You believe me, don't you?"

"I don't think I'm required to answer that," Ironside replied.

"So what now?"

"Just don't leave town," Ironside said.

"You mean I can go?"

"Go," Ironside answered grumpily.

Buckley got up, hesitated a moment, looked at Ed — who looked back at him blankly — then departed.

At the window Ironside remained silent.

Ed Brown began to hum.

"Is that sarcasm?" Ironside asked.

"Whoever heard of a sarcastic hum?"

Ironside wheeled back toward the center of the room. "You didn't believe that guff, did you?" he said.

"That testimonial to your excellence, you mean?" Ed smiled. "Of course I did. It's the latest gimmick in the underworld. If you're innocent, make sure you get Ironside on your case. He always gets the right man. In fact, he's known as the American Royal Mounted Po —"

"All right, all right!" Ironside broke in.

"Didn't you believe it?" Ed asked.

"Maybe. He seemed sincere enough. I don't think he could fake it that well."

"It doesn't do much for your theory that he and Mehl and Jones were working together on it," Ed said.

"It wasn't a theory. It was mere speculation."

"Whatever it was, Mehl and Jones appear to be in the clear now."

Ironside shook his head. "I haven't bought Buckley's story," he said. "It had the ring of truth to it, yes. But even if it is true, it doesn't put Mehl — or Jones, for that matter — in the clear. I still think it's possible that Mehl tried to save Buckley from a life of further crime for some reason other than a desire to be a nice guy. It's possible that, somehow, he's using him."

"Would you like to be a little more specific?" Ed asked with interest.

"Yes, I would like to. But I can't." He looked at his watch. "Where's —"

The door to Ironside's quarters opened, and Mark entered.

"Right on cue," Ed said.

"Not him," Ironside corrected. "I was about to ask where Eve is. How long can she talk to a reporter?"

"It probably depends a lot on whether the reporter is married or single, young or old, charming or a bore," Ed replied.

"Irrelevant," Ironside said. "When Eve is on duty, she sticks strictly to business." He nodded to Mark. "How many garages were you able to hit?"

"A dozen."

"And how many mentions of Tournabeau?"

"Two."

"What's this?" Ed asked.

Ironside told him what he had learned when Mark had telephoned earlier.

"He's a surprise entry," Ed said. "I thought he was
92

a character witness and that was it. How did he get tied in with the paintings?"

"I don't have the answer," Mark said. "So is it okay if I go and get dinner started? If I don't, by the time it's ready it'll be breakfast time."

"Go." Ironside waved.

"Are we having a guest?" Mark asked.

"No, only Ed."

Mark started toward the kitchen.

"Maybe you'd better prepare enough for Eve, too," Ironside called. "She'll probably show up any minute now."

"Got it."

"If I'm not a guest, what am I?" Ed asked.

"What?"

"You said —"

"Oh, that. I don't know what you are. You're unclassifiable." He looked at his watch again. "Did Eve mention that reporter's name?"

"McCandlish," Ed replied. "But leave her alone, will you? You're not her mother."

"Well, she'll probably be popping in in a minute or so." He scowled. "Do you suppose there's some connection between the falling-out of Tuck and Tournabeau and the theft of those paintings?"

"I'm sure about one thing," Ed replied. "It isn't normal behavior when you spend your afternoon going from parking garage to parking garage asking questions about a delivery truck."

"You're right." Ironside nodded. "Somehow there's a definite connection between Tournabeau and the paintings, if not between Tuck and Tournabeau anymore. I wonder. . . ." He wheeled himself toward the pool table. "I wonder if Tournabeau really believes that those paintings were fakes."

"He gave that impression, didn't he?"

"Yes. But, at the time, I put that down as sour grapes. If he really believed it, though, he might be working on the case, hoping to pin something on Tuck." Then he shook his head. "No. I don't think he'd waste his time. He's primarily interested in money. Now that he and Tuck are finished, his sole interest is probably in making another connection."

"You don't think the idea of revenge would appeal to him?" Ed asked.

"Not if —" Ironside made a wry face, then was silent for a few moments, thinking. "But suppose he could combine the two — moneymaking and revenge," he said finally. "Now that, I'd guess, would be right down his alley."

"Blackmail," Ed suggested.

"A possibility that rates a position right at the top of the list," Ironside replied. "If Tournabeau could prove that Tuck arranged for the paintings to be stolen, he might never have to worry about pocket money again."

"How wise would it be to put Tuck over a barrel?" Ed asked.

94

"Very unwise. But Tournabeau probably wouldn't think about that aspect of it. When a blackmailer sees a chance to get his hooks in, nothing deters him."

"The only problem with this theory is that we know that the paintings weren't fakes," Ed pointed out.

"We know it, but — No, let me change that. We assume that the paintings were not fakes. Halverson's reputation seems to be invulnerable. But we're not positive of anything. And, anyway, Tournabeau wouldn't be swayed by what we think. If he has the notion in his head that those paintings are fakes, that's what he'd be working from."

"There's another angle," Ed said. "Maybe the theft had been arranged before Tuck and Tournabeau broke up. Maybe, for some reason, they fought about it. Tuck kicked Tournabeau out, and now Tournabeau wants his cut."

Ironside shook his head. "You belong in fantasyland with Frank Buckley," he said. "Now, think about it. Is that David Tuck's style of operating? He's not a cheap, penny-ante chiseler."

Mark entered from the kitchen, pushing a food cart. "What have I missed?" he asked, heading for the dining table.

"Never mind that," Ironside replied. "What's for dinner?" He sniffed. "Hey! Steak!"

"Somebody'll have to eat Eve's," Mark said, noting that she had not arrived.

"I'll take it," Ironside said. "I'm the one who needs

95

to have his energy cells recharged."

"And I don't?" Ed asked.

"Why should you?" Ironside replied. "You've been asleep practically all day."

It was late evening when Eve appeared. She came in quietly — and smiling bemusedly. Ironside and Ed were in the midst of a game of eight ball. Mark was stretched out in a chair, a mug of coffee on the table beside him.

"That was close," Ironside said, glancing at the clock. "Twenty minutes more and you'd be wearing rags and arriving in a pumpkin."

"It's not the same chick," Mark said, leaning forward. "This one still has both of her slippers."

"Very funny." Eve smiled. She dropped into an easy chair, lolled her head to one side, and, sighing blissfully, removed her shoes.

Ironside turned to Ed. "What is that supposed to mean?" he asked, indicating Eve. "Is that a message in code?"

"I think so," he replied. "I think it means that Mc-Candlish turned out to be young, single, and charming."

Eve reached out an arm, fluttering a long sheet of paper from her fingers. Ed reached out, took it, glanced at it, then handed it to Ironside.

Ironside looked at the type on the length of paper, looked over at Eve, then began reading.

"We went to dinner," Eve explained to Ed.

"Candlelight, wine, et cetera, et cetera?"

"Sort of. We were killing time. He'd already told me the story. He also told me that it would appear in to-morrow morning's paper. But it hadn't been set in type yet."

"So you were killing time — candlelight, wine, et cetera, et cetera."

"Until he could get me a galley proof." She pointed toward the long sheet of paper that Ironside was read-ing. "That's a galley proof," she explained.

Ed's eyes rolled ceilingward. "I know."

Ironside handed the proof to Ed a few moments later. As Ed started to read, Ironside wheeled himself away from the pool table and toward the kitchen.

"Can I get you something?" Mark called after him.

"I'm not a child!" Ironside answered sharply, dis-appearing into the kitchen.

Eve turned to Mark, frowning. "What's he so touchy about?" she asked.

Mark shrugged. "Maybe it was something he read."

When Ed finished the proof, he handed it to Mark. At about the same time Ironside reappeared from the kitchen. He was sipping coffee from a mug and looking annoyed.

"What did I do?" Eve asked. "I thought you'd want that proof."

"You did fine," he replied. "You were right; I did want it. You say the story will be in tomorrow's paper?"

Eve nodded.

"Although it isn't final proof of anything," Ironside said, "it intimates that Tuck's financial empire is falling apart in places. But —" he stopped the wheelchair, sipped the coffee again, then continued — "it doesn't really provide the proof, does it?"

"It read pretty convincingly to me," Ed replied.

"I'm sold," Eve added.

"Let's examine the story," Ironside said. "A number of links in this chain of companies Tuck has put together have shown weakness."

"Heavy losses," Ed corrected. "Not just weakness — heavy losses."

"All right, heavy losses. But that's the whole point of putting all these companies together under one control. When some of them suffer losses, the others can protect them."

"I mentioned that to Roger," Eve said. "He —"

"Who?"

"Roger McCandlish. He said that the problem is that Tuck's other companies aren't that strong. They can't be used to —"

Ironside broke in on her again. "If this two-bit reporter knows so much, how come *he* isn't the multimillionare?" he snapped.

Eve did not answer.

Ed made a sound in his throat.

"All right," Ironside said apologetically. "I suppose McCandlish knows what he's talking about. But, on the other hand, Tuck has been in trouble like this before —

98

a number of times — and he's always pulled himself out of it. Is McCandlish aware of that?"

Eve nodded.

"And he doesn't say the empire is dying," Ironside said. "He says only that it's showing some cracks. That could happen to any business."

"What are we trying to do," Ed asked irritably, "defend David Tuck or find out who stole those paintings?"

"I don't happen to like newspaper reporters who make mountains out of molehills, that's all," Ironside snapped. "It's happened to me a number of times, too."

Mark rattled the galley proof. "I didn't find any molehills in here," he said. "This guy just says this and this and this are happening, that's all. If it isn't true, I guess Tuck can deny it — or sue him or something."

"I'm not saying it isn't true," Ironside said.

"Then what *are* you saying?" Ed asked.

Ironside finished off the mug of coffee. He put the mug on the dining table, then wheeled himself to the window. "I'm saying I'm tired of this case coming up with new surprises every hour on the hour," he replied after a minute.

"I'm glad that's it," Eve said. "I was afraid you were beginning to identify yourself with David Tuck — because you two are so much alike, I mean. If that were happening, you might not want to believe certain things about him."

Ironside turned away from the window. "I think it's time for all of us to turn ourselves off," he said. "We

99

need a rest from this case and some sleep." He waved. "Good night, all."

Ed and Eve rose and started toward the door.

"Eve. . . ."

They stopped and looked back.

Ironside pointed. "Your shoes," he said to Eve.

She returned and picked them up, then, carrying them, left with Ed.

When they had gone, Ironside said to Mark, "Let that be a lesson to you. Always go easy on the candlelight, wine, et cetera."

"That's what's made me what I am today," Mark replied.

Ironside picked up the galley proof again and began reading it for the second time. When he finished, he tossed it aside.

"I was sure that most of what Tournabeau was saying was just talk," he said. "Instinct told me that's what it was."

"If he was right about Tuck's empire — about its being shaky — maybe he was right about those paintings."

"About them being fakes?"

Mark nodded.

"I'm not going to think about it anymore tonight," Ironside decided. "Just thinking about thinking about it boggles the mind."

6 The "Born Winner"

THE FOLLOWING MORNING Ironside sent both Ed Brown and Mark out to pursue the lead that Mark had been pursuing alone the day before — going from parking garage to parking garage, talking to attendants, seeking some indication that the paintings might have been dropped off at one of them.

Meanwhile, he had Eve do some telephoning. She began calling the businessmen to whom she had talked about Tuck a day earlier and getting their reaction to the story in the *Journal*.

"They have mixed ideas about it," Eve reported to Ironside when, close to noon, she completed the final call. "Some think that what McCandlish has found is very significant and that Mr. Tuck is about to be without an empire. But others — the majority, I'd say — were of the opinion that, with a little luck, Mr. Tuck will be able to resolve the problems and put the empire back together the way it was."

"Luck. Whose term is that, yours or theirs?" Ironside asked.

Eve thought for a second, then replied, "I'm not sure. It might be my term, or partly mine and partly theirs. But, either way, it was the impression I got — that Tuck would need some luck." She studied him. "Why is that so important?"

"Oh, no particular reason. Just something that Mark said about luck."

"What?"

"That sometimes when a man needs it, it's out of town."

Eve laughed.

"Let's take a look at this thing," Ironside said, troubled. "We have a man who's had several million dollars' worth of paintings stolen from him, and it seems that, somehow, the man himself has become our prime suspect. How did it happen?"

"It happened when Harry Tournabeau dropped that bomb about the paintings being fakes," Eve replied. "If they are, then Mr. Tuck could have arranged to

102

have the paintings stolen so that he could collect the insurance money, which — maybe — he needs because he's in financial trouble."

"In other words, we're off on this wild-goose chase simply because Harry Tournabeau made an accusation," Ironside said disgustedly. "And Tournabeau, it seems to me, is probably the least trustworthy of all the people we've talked to."

"Well . . . yes . . . but. . . ."

"He's an admitted double crosser," Ironside went on. "He told us himself that he tried to pull a fast one on Tuck."

Eve nodded. "I know. But —"

"And I checked on Alver Halverson's reputation," Ironside continued. "Everybody in his profession — even his competitors — says he's one hundred percent honorable. And Halverson says that those paintings were authentic."

"But there's always a first —"

"Don't give me clichés," Ironside interrupted. "I want facts. Why are we spending so much time on Tuck?"

"His financial problem."

Ironside snorted. "A newspaper story."

"Oh, it's real enough, I'm sure," Eve said. "No one has even suggested that it isn't. There are just different opinions on how it will end."

Ironside was quiet for a few moments. Then he said, "How good are we, collectively, as judges of people?"

Eve smiled. "Sizing them up, you mean?"

"Exactly."

"We have a sort of so-so record, I suppose. Why?"

"Let's get Tuck up here," Ironside said. "Let's put him in a relaxed setting and see how he responds. Maybe he'll tell us some things about himself."

"I thought you were only interested in facts."

"I'm talking about facts — facts about Mr. David Tuck. The solution to this case may depend on those. Is Tuck in such bad condition financially that he needs the insurance money from those paintings to save himself? Would he be capable of buying a pass for some fake paintings?"

"But you've already decided that the paintings *aren't* fakes," Eve argued.

"I haven't. I simply pointed out that it's unlikely that they are. Halverson doesn't seem to be the kind who can be bought. But there's always a first time for everything."

"When I started to say that, it was a cliché," Eve objected.

"Don't be difficult," Ironside grumbled. "Get on the phone. Tuck hinted around about wanting an invitation to look this place over, didn't he? All right, let's take the hint. Invite him to dinner. Tell him we're having chili and to come prepared for poker and eight ball afterward."

"He'd be a fool to turn down an offer like that." Eve smiled as she reached for the phone.

104

When Mark called early in the afternoon, Ironside ordered him back to Headquarters to prepare a pot of chili, informing him that David Tuck would be their guest for dinner that evening.

"Chili?" Mark asked. "That man's a millionaire who lives in a castle, and you invited him up for chili?"

"We're not so sure he's still a millionaire," Ironside replied. "But, millionaire or not, he's a normal human male, isn't he? If he is, chili is his favorite dish."

"How do you figure that?"

"Because it happens to be my favorite. Now, will you get back here and put the pot on?"

Mark returned, and the pot was put on. A while later Ed phoned in. He had completed the survey of parking garages, but he had turned up no indication that the truck carrying the crated paintings had dropped them off at any of them. Ironside ordered him to return to Headquarters.

"I guess it wasn't a complete waste of time," Ed said when he returned. "We can forget about Tournabeau now. He undoubtedly found out the same thing Mark and I did. With nothing to go on, I assume he'll discard the idea that the paintings were stashed at a garage."

"The weakness there is that we're not positive of what Tournabeau learned," Ironside said. "He might have talked to an attendant who saw something. I think it would be a good idea for you to go to Tournabeau's hotel tomorrow and question him. The chances are that he didn't find out any more than you and Mark did,

105

but let's not be too sure about it until we've checked on him."

"Will do," Ed nodded.

The evening, in one way, was a success. David Tuck arrived exactly on time. He claimed to like Ironside's quarters better than his own castle. Chili, he announced when it was served, was his favorite dish, and he had three helpings. After dinner, while the others watched, Ironside and Tuck played a game of eight ball. When only the eight ball itself was left on the table, Ironside won by sinking it with a bank shot. After that, the entire group — Tuck, Ironside, Eve, Mark, and Ed — settled down for a few hands of poker. The game continued into the wee hours of morning — with Eve, assisted by luck, ending up the big winner, with a gain of thirteen cents.

Tuck was fully at ease during the entire evening and, encouraged by the others, talked a great deal about himself. The stories he told concerned his early days in business.

"I knew when I was a very young man that I was destined to make it big," he said. "I've worked hard and, as I mentioned to you once, I believe, I've paid close attention to detail. But a lot of what I've accomplished has been handed to me, too. I admit it. And I think it's because I was always intended to succeed."

"Fate?" Ironside asked.

"Give it whatever name you want," Tuck replied. "All I can say is that I've always had this feeling that

I couldn't possibly fail. Oh, I've had some setbacks. I'm having a few right now. But, in the end, I've always advanced."

"I saw that story in the *Journal*," Ironside said. "Was it accurate?"

"Totally true. Absolutely factual," Tuck replied. "At the same time, however, it was also wholly misleading."

"How, exactly, could that be?" Ironside asked.

"It's true that a number of my companies are in trouble," Tuck replied. "The impression the story gave — that my entire operation is falling apart — couldn't be more false, however."

"Mr. McCandlish didn't exactly say that your whole operation is falling apart, Mr. Tuck," Eve said.

"Wasn't that the impression the piece gave, though?"

"I thought so," Ironside agreed. "I'm happy to learn it isn't true."

"I'll always be on top," Tuck said. "And I'll tell you why. It's because I'm very careful about choosing the men I do business with."

"Only the honest ones?" Eve guessed.

"On the contrary. I steer clear of honest businessmen. The big profit is in dealing with those who are trying to outsmart you. The secret, of course, is in knowing that they're trying to fast-shuffle you and in outsmarting them first."

There was silence for a moment.

"Isn't that dangerous?" Ironside said finally. "It's gambling, in a sense, isn't it?"

"Of course it is."

"We gamble here, playing poker," Ironside went on, "but for small stakes. This evening, for instance, we played for several hours — and the big winner ended up with a profit of thirteen cents. You deal in millions, though."

"And in survival as a businessman," Ed said.

"That's true," Tuck said. "I have something going for me that the others don't have, however. In fact, I have two things. Number one, I usually know that they're trying to outsmart me, but they don't realize I know it. And number two — the most important element — I'm a born winner." He grinned broadly. "I sometimes doubt that I could lose even if I tried."

Once more the room became silent.

"You don't believe me, do you?" Tuck smiled challengingly at his listeners.

"It's just that it's — uh — sort of tempting the gods to make a statement like that," Ed said. "It makes people nervous."

Tuck laughed. "Chief Ironside doesn't look very nervous. I'd guess he's a born winner, too."

"I've never made that claim," Ironside responded, "and I certainly wouldn't make it tonight. Three of those pennies that Eve won were mine." He cocked his head slightly to the right, studying Tuck. "She ended up with a few of your pennies, too," he said. "How does a born winner account for that?"

"Tonight gambling was a game," Tuck replied.

"When the stakes are high, it's a business. Then I rarely lose."

"Rarely? That's a little different from never."

"As I told you before, I occasionally have temporary setbacks," Tuck said, "but they're never serious." He rose from his chair. "Well, it's been pleasant — very, very pleasant — but I don't want to keep you up any longer."

Tuck shook hands all around, expressed his appreciation for the invitation once again, and departed.

"Well?" Ironside queried the others.

"He's building himself up for a fall," Eve said.

"I wouldn't bet any of my good money on that," Ironside replied. "He's probably been saying for years that he can't be beaten. And other people have undoubtedly been reacting in a perfectly normal way — predicting that he was building himself up for a fall. But has he fallen? No. He's cocky, true, but that doesn't mean that he's destined eventually to fail."

"I agree," Ed said. "I think we can forget this idea that Tuck arranged for the paintings to be stolen so he could collect the insurance money. He convinced me that he's unbeatable. If I had any money to invest, I'd put it in Tuck's companies."

"I feel exactly the same way about that aspect of it," Ironside said. "Let's forget this idea that Tuck's empire is crumbling. Don't forget that the notion came first from Tournabeau, a man that Tuck had dismissed. And then we fed it on information we received from men who had done business with him. We know now that those men probably tried to outsmart him and ended up being outsmarted themselves. They would probably like to believe that he's in real trouble."

"But there's also McCandlish's story," Eve reminded him.

"Tuck explained that. The story simply gave the wrong impression."

"Tuck is in the clear, then?" Eve asked.

"As far as I'm concerned, he is," Ironside replied. "Any arguments?"

There was no reply.

"He's a nice chap," Ironside said. "We'll have to invite him back again. I feel a little sorry for him, though."

"Yeah, poor guy," Ed said. "He has nothing but money."

"No, that's not what I mean. He's probably happy, in his own way, with money. It's apparently what he wants. He couldn't be very happy, though, with his way of getting it."

"What do you mean?" Eve asked.

"Obviously he spends his time looking for dishonest businessmen," Ironside replied. "They're the kind he makes money on — by outsmarting them before they outsmart him."

"So?" Ed said.

"He must have a pretty poor opinion of people," Ironside replied. "He probably thinks we're *all* crooked."

7 Too Many Suspects

AFTER NOT MUCH sleep Ironside was in an unpleasant mood the next morning. He complained about the coffee, which had been made the same way as always. A while later, when Ed and Eve arrived at his quarters ready for assignment, he let them sit for nearly an hour before he gave them so much as a good-morning.

The mood was broken when a relieved smile suddenly broke across Ironside's face. "Of course!" he said, speaking to himself.

"Look! It talks!" Mark said.

112

"How!" Ironside grinned. "That's what we want."

"That's what I've been telling them down at the office," Ed replied.

"Not *who*. What we want is *how*," Ironside went on, ignoring the comments from Ed and Mark. "We've been concentrating on trying to find out *who* stole those paintings. But I suspect that if we figure out *how*, we'll automatically discover *who*." He turned to Eve. "First, call the auction house. Find out if Buckley and Jones are back at work. If they are, tell them we'll want them at the Tuck mansion this morning, and ask them to stand by. Then call Tuck and find out when he'll be available. The point is, I want all three of them — Tuck, Buckley, and Jones — there together."

Happy to be back in action, Eve moved to the telephone.

"Ed," Ironside commanded, "go talk to Tournabeau. Maybe he found out something, talking to those garage attendants, that we didn't. If he did, get it out of him."

"I'm on my way," Ed said, striding toward the door.

A few minutes later Eve reported that Tuck would be available all morning and that Buckley and Jones were already on their way to the mansion to meet Ironside. Ironside, Eve, and Mark left Headquarters at once.

When they reached the Tuck mansion, they saw the auction house truck parked outside the entrance. Buckley and Jones got out to meet them.

"Mr. Mehl told us to get right out here," Buckley

113

informed Ironside. "He said we should do anything you want, Chief."

"Good. What I want you to do is some remembering," Ironside replied. Then, without explaining further, he led the way toward the entrance.

David Tuck was just stepping off the elevator as they reached it. "Sorry I wasn't out there to meet you, Chief," he said. "Mrs. Alcorn told me you'd arrived, but I was on the phone. What is it? What game are we playing today? Anything interesting?"

"As interesting as eight ball, I assume you mean," Ironside replied. "Well, to me it is. It may be a little dull for the participants, though. What I want you to do is to go through the motions of what you did the day of the theft."

"The whole day?" Tuck asked.

"From the time Buckley and Jones arrived," Ironside answered.

"Well, I met them here. . . ." Tuck began.

"That's right," Buckley agreed.

"Right here, almost to the spot," Jones said.

"And from here we went to the room where the paintings were stored," Tuck said. He opened the elevator door. "Shall we go up?"

The entire group got into the car, then Tuck closed the door and punched the button.

"Who supplied the packing material?" Ironside asked.

Tuck laughed. "Is that important?"

Ironside shrugged. "It might be . . . it might not be."

114

"We brought our own stuff," Buckley said.

"That's right," Jones agreed. "We went up, and then we went back and got it. Do you want us to do that?"

Ironside shook his head.

Tuck chuckled. "I hope you don't mind if I find some of this amusing," he said to Ironside. "Doing it all again, step by step, seems a little . . . well . . . ah . . . a little. . . ."

"Like something out of a mystery novel?"

"Yes."

"I'm willing to look a little foolish," Ironside said.

"I just don't see —"

The elevator door was opening, and Ironside was wheeling himself out. "Where to from here?" he asked.

Tuck took the lead and led the way down the corridor. "I had the paintings in a room down here," he said.

"This is where it was, all right," Buckley affirmed. "Look at them doors. Nobody could forget them doors. With all that iron trim and crosspieces on them, they look like they weigh a ton."

"Impressive." Ironside nodded.

"But they look like the doors on the other floors," Mark said.

"That's true," Tuck said. "Most of the doors in the castle are like this. Not all the rooms are the same, however." He halted at a door. "This is where I had the paintings," he said.

"Let's go in," Ironside suggested.

Tuck opened the door and they entered. The room was fair-sized. There were lengths of cord, pieces of board, and what looked like insulating material on the floor.

"That's the stuff we brought, some of it," Buckley said. "This is the room." He looked around. "Yeah, I'd know it."

Ironside turned to Jones. "Do you agree?"

"I'll tell you in a second," Jones said.

He went to a window, bent down, then straightened. "This is the place, okay," he said. He pointed. "The glass here, it's got a little chip out of it. I remember that."

"Good."

"I don't believe I understand this," Tuck said. "Of course this is the room. I told you that when I brought you here. Why is there a need for confirmation?"

"Just double-checking," Ironside replied. "I learned it reading mystery novels. Now, you reached here, then the packing began. Is that right?"

"Nope. First we went and got our packing material," Buckley answered. "Then, after that, after we brought it up, the packing started" — he glanced at Tuck — "with Mr. Tuck telling us how to do it."

"Yes, I supervised," Tuck acknowledged.

Ironside addressed Buckley. "Did Mr. Tuck give you any special instructions?"

Buckley thought for a minute. "How do you mean that?" he asked finally.

116

Tuck chuckled again.

"Did he have you do anything that you wouldn't have normally done?"

Buckley pondered again, then shook his head. "All he did was, he kept an eye on us and told us how he wanted it done and, you know, where to put the crates and like that."

"That's all," Jones agreed.

"Where to put the crates?" Ironside asked.

"Over there against the wall," Buckley replied, pointing. "We'd pack them, then we'd put the crates over there."

"To get them out of the way," Tuck said to Ironside. "We were doing it efficiently, that's all."

"Is there anything else about the packing that stands out in your minds?" Ironside asked Buckley and Jones.

They both shook their heads immediately.

"Think about it," Ironside urged.

"Chief," Tuck said, "I'm sure you have a logical reason for doing this. But for the life of me I can't figure out what it is. Could you enlighten me?"

"I simply want to know how those paintings were stolen," Ironside replied.

"Naturally. But they weren't stolen here. The theft occurred while the truck was on its way into the city."

"I'm quite aware of that," Ironside said. "It's possible that preparations were made — that the scene was set, so to speak — for the theft while the paintings were still here."

117

"Oh." Tuck nodded. He seemed not really to understand, however.

"Well?" Ironside said to Buckley and Jones.

Buckley shook his head. "That's it," he insisted. "We packed the paintings and stacked the crates over there. That's it — period."

"I don't remember nothing else," Jones said.

"All right," Ironside said. "We'll assume that the paintings have been packed and the crates have been stacked. What next?"

"We went up and signed the receipt," Buckley said.

Ironside gestured toward the door. "Let's go."

They left the room, returned to the elevator, ascended to the next floor, and walked along the corridor to Tuck's office.

Mrs. Alcorn, at her desk, looked up as they entered.

"Here's the place," Buckley said to Ironside. "And that's the same lady."

"Unless she's got a twin," Jones said.

Tuck sighed. "Is this going to take much longer, Chief?"

"Probably not." He spoke to Buckley. "And you say Mr. Tuck dictated the wording of the receipt while you waited?"

Buckley looked puzzled. "I didn't say that."

"How *did* it happen, then?"

"We just come in, and Mr. Tuck said to give me the receipt. I signed it and we went."

"The receipt was already typed up?"

"That's right," Tuck said. "And with two carbons. Is there something suspicious about that, Chief?"

"On the contrary," Ironside replied. He addressed Buckley again. "Were you here long enough, would you say, for someone to remove those crates from that room?" he asked.

Buckley frowned. "Not unless he was Superman," he replied. "We had fifty-seven crates, and they was all heavy. Some was heavier than others, but none of them could be picked up a couple at a time." He shook his head. "Nobody could have got them crates out of there."

"Now, there is a question I truly don't understand," Tuck said. "We *know* no one moved the crates, because they were there when we returned. Chief, you baffle me. I can't follow your line of thinking."

"What the Chief is getting at —" Eve began.

"Please," Ironside broke in. "The magician never explains his tricks. That takes the magic out of it."

Tuck laughed again. "I think I understand it now," he said. "You just keep asking questions, whether they're relevant or not, until someone gives a wrong answer. Then that's your man, right?"

"Something like that, I suppose," Ironside replied vaguely. He spoke to Buckley again. "How long were you here, would you say? Five minutes? Ten minutes?"

"Not that long. As long as it takes to write my name, that's all."

"Didn't you read what you signed?"

"Oh, sure. But it was only a couple of lines."

"Then back to the room where the paintings were waiting?"

"Right," Buckley replied.

"Jones?"

"That's it," the younger man said. "A couple minutes, that's all we was here."

"Let's hit the road," Ironside said.

They left Tuck's office, descended in the elevator, then moved once more toward the room where the paintings had been packed.

"These paintings here, hanging in this corridor, are they reproductions, too?" Ironside asked Tuck.

Tuck dropped back to walk beside Ironside, and Buckley took the lead.

"Yes, most of them," Tuck replied. "And the ones that are originals aren't valuable. Are you able to discern the difference between the real paintings and the reproductions?"

"Well, the light isn't too good along here," Ironside replied.

Tuck started to point to one of the paintings, then he abruptly changed his mind and called to Buckley, who had started to open a door.

"No, no, one more door," Tuck said.

"That's right." Buckley nodded. "It *was* the next." He moved on, then opened the door to the room next in line along the corridor. "Here it is."

They all entered the room. Ironside wheeled himself to the window and looked out. "I can see the truck and

120

the paddy wagon down there," he said. "In fact, they're almost directly below."

There was silence from the others.

"Just mentioning it." Ironside smiled, facing them again. "At this point," he said, "the paintings had been packed and were ready to be taken to the truck. Is that right?"

"That's it," Buckley replied.

"*All* of the paintings? Nothing was left till the last minute?"

"All fifty-seven of them," Buckley answered. "Mr. Tuck made sure we were all set to move."

"Efficiency." Tuck smiled.

"And Mr. Tuck left you then?" Ironside said to Buckley.

"No, sir. He stayed with us right to the end."

Ironside looked at Tuck.

"Wouldn't you have stayed with it right to the end, Chief?" Tuck asked.

"Mmmmmm." Ironside addressed Buckley again. "Did he accompany a painting each time it was taken down to the truck?"

"No."

"I couldn't have been with both of them, could I?" Tuck said. "While Buckley was going, Jones was coming. I'd have had to be two people."

"Just asking." Ironside smiled. "Well, I suppose we've seen all there is to see here. Shall we follow the trail from here to the truck?"

They left the room and turned toward the elevator.

On the way Ironside, lowering his voice, said to Mark, "I'll arrange to separate Jones and Buckley. Talk to Jones — talk to him casually. He may let something slip."

"Like what?"

"How would I know? How could I possibly know before he lets it slip?"

They reached the elevator and descended to the main floor. From there they moved outside.

"Where, exactly, was the truck parked?" Ironside asked Buckley.

"Right here. Right here by the door."

"Not where it is now, then? In other words, I might not have been able to see it, when I looked out of that window, if it had been parked where it was the day of the theft?"

"Well, I don't know about that," Buckley replied. "I wasn't looking out the window. I was busy carrying them paintings down."

"You refer to them as the 'paintings,' " Ironside said. "But by then they were in crates. I wonder why you didn't say you were carrying the 'crates.' "

Obviously bothered, Buckley looked at Jones, who looked baffled.

"I don't know why I said it that way," Buckley answered. "I wasn't thinking about what I was saying; I was just saying."

"Maybe it's not important." Ironside smiled. He

looked upward. "Mr. Tuck was in that room all the time, though, wasn't he?" he said. "So he might have looked out the window."

"Yes, if I'd wanted to look out the window, I might have looked out the window," Tuck said testily. "But, as I recall, I had no great desire to look out windows that day. Would you mind telling us, Chief, what possible difference it could make whether or not I could see the truck from that window?"

Ironside shrugged. "Probably none," he answered.

"Then why does the possibility fascinate you so much?"

"Fascinate me? It doesn't. I was just asking another of those irrelevant questions." He turned to Buckley. "I'd like to know exactly how long it took you to transport a crate from the room to the truck," he said. "Go through the motions, I'll time you."

Buckley started to go back into the house, then stopped. "How will you know when I'm ready to start?" he asked.

Ironside looked up. "Signal to us from that window," he suggested.

Buckley nodded, then disappeared into the castle.

"I want to do this right," Ironside said to Jones. "Open the back of the truck. I'll have Frank go through the motions of putting a crate into it, too."

Jones walked toward the truck. A moment later Mark tagged after him.

"Police work is fascinating," Ironside said to Tuck.

123

"That is, if you have a great deal of patience."

"Apparently I don't," Tuck replied.

"What a joke it would be if we discovered in the end that we'd been wasting all our time," Ironside said. "If we discovered, for instance, that the paintings were fakes — and worthless."

Tuck glanced at his watch. "What's taking him so long?"

"Doesn't that theory pique your interest at all?" Ironside asked.

Tuck looked at him. "What theory?"

"The idea that the paintings might be fakes."

"Oh, that. I didn't take that seriously. I thought you were just making conversation." He shook his head. "No, it doesn't pique my interest," he said. "The paintings were authenticated by a man who does not make mistakes. He —" He pointed upward. "There's Buckley. He's waving."

"Wave back," Ironside ordered.

Tuck obeyed. Ironside looked at his watch. Several minutes later Frank Buckley reappeared, and Ironside asked him to continue to the truck and pretend to be loading a crate into it. He followed instructions, then returned, accompanied by Jones and Mark.

"Fine, fine," Ironside said to Buckley. "I think that will be all. And thank you for your cooperation."

"I hope it helped," Buckley said.

"We'll see. . . ."

Buckley and Jones got into the truck and drove off.

"I won't take up any more of your time," Ironside said to Tuck. "You probably have other things to do."

"Yes," Tuck replied, a little irritably. "I didn't realize this would take so much time. So if you'll excuse me. . . ."

"Again, thank you for your cooperation."

Tuck hurried toward the entrance doorway. Ironside, watching him go, smiled in a satisfied way to himself. Then he signaled to Mark to lower the lift.

Ironside was still smiling his satisfied smile when, a while later, the paddy wagon left the Tuck property and turned onto the parkway that led back to the city.

"I give up," Eve said. "What is it you know that I don't know?"

"Absolutely nothing — well, with one minor exception. I know that the principal suspects don't know that I don't know anything more than I did before."

Eve looked pained. "You mean all that up and down and in and out and waving from windows and timing Buckley — You mean all that was for nothing?"

"Did you learn anything?"

"No."

"I didn't, either," Ironside said. "But our suspects don't know that, do they?"

Eve sighed. "I don't know," she replied. "It's just possible that —"

"Don't confuse matters any more than they are," Ironside said, breaking in.

At that moment the phone rang. Ironside picked it up. Ed Brown was calling.

"I phoned you twice before but didn't get any answer," Ed began.

"We've been away from the van, playing games," Ironside answered with a chuckle. "Why were you calling?"

"My luck hasn't been the best. When I arrived at the hotel I was told that Tournabeau was out. I sat down in the lobby, and the clerk was supposed to let me know when Tournabeau came in. Apparently, though, Tournabeau came in a side or rear entrance, bypassing the desk, because about an hour later I saw him leaving. I ran to catch up with him, but I was too late. He got into his car and drove off."

"And now he's gone," Ironside finished for him.

"Yes and no. I got into my own car and started to follow him. But, as I said, this isn't my lucky day. I got a flat."

"Then I was right — he's gone."

"Maybe not. He was headed toward Tuck's estate. I got the flat just as he was turning onto the parkway. If you're there, or on your way back, you might see him. You couldn't miss him. He's driving a white Caddy convertible."

"All right," Ironside said. "We'll keep an eye out. Is your flat fixed?"

"Yes," Ed answered.

"Drive back to the hotel and stake it out," Ironside directed. "If we miss him, you'll be able to catch him, I hope, when he returns."

126

When he hung up, Ironside called up to Mark and asked him to keep a lookout for a white Cadillac convertible. Then he and Eve began discussing all that had happened at the castle, trying to find some clue that would lead them to the solution of the case.

"We're going to leave the parkway," Mark called.

"And you haven't seen that convertible?" Ironside asked, surprised. "Do you suppose it passed us before I told you to start looking for it?"

"How could a white Cadillac convertible get by me, whether I was looking for it or not?" Mark asked.

"You're right. Pull over. Let me work on this."

The paddy wagon stopped on the shoulder of the parkway.

"If he didn't drive past us, where did he go?" Ironside asked.

"Maybe Ed was wrong," Eve suggested. "Maybe he wasn't headed this way."

"That's possible. But suppose he wasn't wrong. It's possible that Tournabeau arrived at the Tuck estate before we left. That way, we wouldn't meet him on the road."

"But we didn't see him there."

"Tournabeau was Tuck's right-hand man," Ironside said. "He would know how to get into and out of the grounds without using the gate." He spoke to Mark. "Turn this ark around. Let's play a hunch. I think Tournabeau is back at the Tuck estate."

Mark drove back onto the parkway, left it by an exit,

then drove back onto it and headed back in the direction of David Tuck's castle.

When they reached the gate, Ironside asked the guard if he had seen Tournabeau or the white Cadillac. The answer was no. Ironside ordered Mark to drive on to the main building.

As they reached it, Ironside suggested to Eve that she go up to Tuck's office and tell him that he might soon be receiving a visit from Tournabeau.

"Then we'll wait around awhile and see what happens," he said.

Just as Eve stepped down from the van, the crackle of gunshots was heard from inside the castle. Eve, barely pausing, raced toward the entrance, drawing her gun.

"Get in there!" Ironside snapped to Mark.

Mark ran after Eve and disappeared into the castle immediately behind her.

It was a long, irritating wait for Ironside, because absolutely nothing appeared to be happening. Eventually, however, Eve and Mark reappeared, accompanied by David Tuck.

"I suppose I ought to thank you," Tuck said grudgingly, "but help wasn't really necessary. I handled it by myself."

"I'm glad to hear that," Ironside replied gruffly. "But you handled *what* by yourself?"

"Someone broke into his private files," Eve explained. "Mr. Tuck caught him at it and fired at him."

"Was it Tournabeau?"

"Of course not," Tuck replied. "I'd know Harry. This was a stranger ... an older man ... a professional, I suppose. Harry Tournabeau would never show up here again."

"A stranger — but he knew exactly where to go to find your private files?"

"Pure chance," Tuck said. "Besides, it's not important. Nothing is gone. He was at the file, but he didn't get into it. I spotted him and took a few shots at him."

"Did you hit him?"

Tuck shook his head. "I don't think he'll be back, though. I must have scared him."

"We'll send someone out to investigate it," Ironside said.

"Forget it, Chief," Tuck said. "Believe me, it isn't important."

"I'll have to report it."

"All right, report it if you must, but don't make a big thing out of it. All I'll get out of it is a lot of publicity that I don't need. Just drop it."

"I'll think about it," Ironside said. He motioned to Mark and Eve. "We can go, I suppose," he said.

Without another word Tuck turned and went back into the castle.

"If you ask me, there goes a bothered man," Mark said.

"I agree," Eve said.

"That makes it unanimous," Ironside said with a nod.

Mark and Eve got back into the paddy wagon; Mark

129

started the engine, then steered toward the gate.

"Did you see that file?" Ironside asked Eve.

"No. I got my information — most of it — from his secretary. She was in the outer office and she told me what had happened. Then Tuck came out. I never did get into his office."

"What do you think?"

"Tournabeau was here. He broke into Tuck's private file and stole something."

"That's the way I see it," Ironside said. "I wonder, though. Does it have anything to do with the paintings?"

Eve looked suddenly disappointed. "It didn't occur to me that it might involve something else," she said.

"It could have been anything. Still. . . ."

They were leaving the Tuck estate and driving back onto the parkway. Ironside reached for the phone.

"I want to know what Tournabeau got — if he got something," Ironside said.

"How —"

"Just a second," Ironside interrupted.

He had reached the number he was calling — the hotel at which Tournabeau was registered. He talked to the clerk, learned that Ed Brown had returned and was seated in the lobby, then had Ed called to the phone.

Without any explanation, Ironside told Ed abruptly, "I think Tournabeau will be showing up there soon. Let him go to his room. But don't let him leave again. I'm on my way, and I want to talk to him."

"What happened?" Ed asked.

130

"I have an idea that Tournabeau has been doing some second-story work. When he left, was he carrying anything?"

"Nope. Empty-handed." Ed's tone was curious now.

"Take note of what he might be carrying when he returns. That's all."

"Right," Ed replied.

"So far it's been a good day," Ironside said to Eve. "We've added another genuine, honest-to-gosh suspect to the list. Just what we needed."

"Great day." She nodded glumly.

8   A Self-Appointed Genius

WHEN THEY REACHED the hotel, Ironside, Eve, and Mark went into the lobby. Ed, who was seated near the desk, saw them enter. He got up and joined them, looking rather satisfied.

"Did he show?" Ironside asked.

"Right on cue," Ed replied.

"Was he carrying anything?"

"A manila folder. Is that what you expected?"

"I wasn't sure what it would be," Ironside replied. "But a manila folder seems logical, since — if I'm right

— he just robbed a file." He glanced toward the elevators. "All right . . . Ed . . . Eve . . . wait for me in the paddy wagon," he said. "Mark, you come with me."

"Shouldn't one of us go with you?" Eve asked.

"I don't want this to look too much like a storming of the gates. We don't really have anything on Tournabeau — except a hunch." He shook his head. "No, you wait for me."

Ed and Eve headed for the van as Ironside and Mark moved toward the elevators. A few minutes later the two men reached the door of Tournabeau's suite. Mark knocked.

There was no response.

Mark knocked again, this time with more force.

After a second, Tournabeau's voice was heard. He asked who was knocking. His voice sounded acutely irritated. When Ironside answered, Tournabeau's tone changed immediately. In a cordial voice he advised Ironside that he would be at the door "in a minute."

A number of minutes passed.

Mark started to knock again, but Ironside stopped him.

Then the door opened. Tournabeau looked studiedly cool, calm, and collected. He smiled broadly, obviously forcing himself, and gestured elaborately, inviting Ironside and Mark into the suite.

"I was taking a nap. You surprised me," Tournabeau said.

"Quick work," Ironside replied, "since you got back

133

only about ten minutes ago. You must be the kind who can lie down and drop off just like" — he snapped his fingers — "that."

"Well . . . yes, as a matter of fact."

"And come alive just as quickly," Ironside commented. "You certainly don't look as if you'd been napping. Marvelous how you can do it."

Tournabeau's cordiality disappeared. "What do you want, Chief?" he asked sharply.

Ironside looked at him levelly. "The folder."

For a second it seemed that Tournabeau was going to try to carry through the bluff. But then his confidence collapsed. He turned away, avoiding Ironside's gaze, and walked toward a small table that held a humidor of cigars.

"The folder," Ironside said again.

"There are folders and there are folders," Tournabeau replied, selecting a cigar.

"Shall I charge you with breaking, entering, and robbery? Shall I take you to the station and then come back here and search the place?"

Tournabeau was trying to light the cigar, but he was having difficulty connecting it with the flame of the lighter.

"Or will you hand over the folder?" Ironside went on.

Tournabeau put down the cigar and the lighter. "All I took was what belonged to me," he said aggressively. "I had some personal papers in that file, that's all. I knew Tuck wouldn't give them to me. If I wanted them,

134

I knew I'd have to go after them. And I almost got myself killed. Isn't that enough? What more do you want from me?"

"Something closer to the truth would be preferable."

"That *is* the truth."

"May I use your phone?" Ironside said. "A call to Mr. Tuck will settle this. If he says you took your own private papers, then that'll end it."

"All right, all right," Tournabeau replied, surrendering. "I admit it. I took some papers that belong to Tuck — but not because I wanted them for myself. The fact is, Chief, I'm trying to help you. The papers concern those stolen paintings."

Ironside held out a hand.

Tournabeau hesitated, then he sighed and went to a chair, lifted the cushion, and produced a manila folder. He handed it to Ironside.

The papers in the folder were a record of the paintings. They showed that Tuck had purchased them all at the same time from a man named Paul Drum. There were also papers showing that each of the paintings had been authenticated by Alver Halverson.

"Paul Drum?" Ironside asked.

"The name means nothing to me," Tournabeau replied evenly.

Ironside wheeled himself to a table that held a phone, then called the paddy wagon and spoke to Ed Brown. He ordered him to check the name Paul Drum through the records.

135

When he hung up, Ironside faced Tournabeau again. "What more do you know about this?" he asked.

"Nothing much. Only what you know."

"Tell me exactly how much you know," Ironside insisted.

"I didn't know whom Tuck bought them from," Tournabeau replied. "He told me about it, in an off-hand way, but I didn't pay a great deal of attention. He bought the paintings as a 'package,' I knew. Someone — Drum, I suppose — had discovered them. They were under some overpaintings."

"Some what?"

"As the story went, the originals, the valuable canvases, had been painted over so that they looked like run-of-the-mill work. This person — whom I now assume to be Drum — was cleaning them when he discovered the overpainting. He got in touch with Tuck, knowing Tuck was a collector, and Tuck bought them from him."

"As a 'package.' "

"Right."

Ironside grunted, then fell silent, thinking.

"I wanted to help you," Tournabeau said. "I thought the file might turn up something that you could use."

There was no reply from Ironside.

"You can't arrest a man for trying to help the police." Tournabeau's tone began to sound anxious.

Ironside smiled dryly. "Of course not," he replied. "I'm a little curious, though. If you stole that file to

136

give it to me, why did you bring it here? I'm usually at police headquarters."

"I didn't know what was in it. I wanted to study it first. It might not have been any help to you."

"Do you think it *has* helped?"

"Well, it's . . . I don't know."

Ironside smiled again. "We thank you for your interest, anyway," he said. "It's private citizens like you, Tournabeau — the ones who are so determined to help us — who make us feel appreciated. I'll, uh . . . I'll keep this folder. After all, you got it for me, not for yourself. I'll see that it gets back to Mr. Tuck."

"You're not going to take me in?"

Ironside's eyes opened wide. "Take you in? You said yourself that a man can't be arrested for trying to help the police. Why would I take you in?" He turned and wheeled himself toward the door. "But I wouldn't leave town if I were you," he said. "We might need you to *help* us again."

When Ironside and Mark reached the paddy wagon a few minutes later, Ironside called a conference. Ironside told Eve and Ed what had occurred in Tournabeau's suite, then asked Ed if he had found out anything about Paul Drum.

"He's an artist," Ed reported. "He's been booked a couple times. He was charged both times with fraud, but he wasn't convicted either time." He handed Ironside a slip of paper. "This is his last known address."

"That's not far from here," Ironside said, looking at

137

Ed's note. "Let's see if he still lives there." He passed the slip of paper back to Ed. "Give it to Mark," he said.

After a few moments the van pulled away from the curb.

"We can be pretty sure, I suppose, that Tournabeau wasn't really trying to help us," Ed said. "So what *did* he have in mind?"

"Blackmail," Eve answered.

Ironside nodded agreement.

"Tournabeau is convinced that those paintings are fakes," Eve continued. "If he could prove it, he might be able to get David Tuck to pay him to keep quiet."

"All right, that's Tournabeau's hang-up," Ed said. "But why are we letting it lead *us* around? We know the paintings aren't fakes."

"Do we?" Eve said. "Before, we were fairly sure they weren't. But, now — I don't think we can be so positive anymore. Look at the evidence. The paintings were bought as a 'package,' and from a man who has been charged twice with fraud."

"Charged, not convicted," Ironside reminded her. "There's a considerable difference, you know."

"But a 'package' deal?"

"I don't think there's really anything suspicious about that," Ironside said. "The canvases were painted over. That means that someone at sometime knew their value and wanted to keep it hidden. It could have happened, say, during a war, when the owner of the paintings

138

wanted to keep them from catching the interest of the invaders. He would have painted them *all* over, wouldn't he? And, more than likely, he would have kept them together." He shook his head. "It wouldn't be the first time for that."

"But how did Drum get them, all in a package like that?" Eve insisted.

"Somebody, someday, was bound to discover the real canvases beneath the overpaintings. Why not Drum?"

"It just seems to me that —"

"We don't know the man, Eve," Ironside interrupted. "Let's not find him guilty just because he's been charged with fraud. I repeat, he was not convicted."

"I think I suggested this before — somebody did, anyway," Ed said. "Isn't it possible that this squabble between Tuck and Tournabeau is all put on?"

Ironside looked at him thoughtfully.

"Let's take this robbery," Ed said. "Tournabeau claimed he was going to turn over to us what he found. We assumed — naturally, I suppose — that he was lying. But maybe that's what he did intend to do, and for a very good reason."

"You lost me a long time ago," Eve said.

"Well, we have what was in the folder," Ed said. "But what, actually, do we have?"

"A new lead."

"What we have is information that Tuck bought the paintings from a man named Drum and that he bought them as a package. But the Chief has just told us that both of these items of information are practically worthless. There's no reason why Drum couldn't have found valuable canvases under overpaintings, and there's no reason why he couldn't have sold them to Tuck in one lump. My point is that there's nothing really suspicious about either factor."

"We're not sure of that," Eve argued.

"I'll grant you that," Ed admitted. "What, though, is the one thing that all this has proved to us?"

Eve looked blank.

"I think I see what Ed is getting at," Ironside said. "It's obvious, Eve, if you think about it a minute. Let me put it another way. Who, among the principals, is not now a suspect?"

"Well . . . not. . . ." She brightened. "Yes, I see. We're not thinking about Tournabeau as the possible thief anymore. He seems to be trying as hard as we are to find out who stole the paintings, only he's concentrating on Tuck."

"That's it," Ed said. "Suppose Tuck is in big trouble with his business interests and needs cash fast. He has these fake paintings. He knows that if he puts them on the legitimate market it will be discovered that they're worthless. So he works out a plan with his right-hand man, Tournabeau. They'll appear to split. Tournabeau will handle the theft of the paintings. Then he'll peddle them in the underworld market. He'll get a good price for them because, with all the publicity, it will be assumed that they're genuine. And, on top of that, Tuck will get the insurance money. In other words, he'll get the cash he badly needs to pull his business interests out of the hole."

Ironside shook his head. "Very dramatic — but unlikely," he said.

"Why? Why?" Ed and Eve asked together.

"Too complicated . . . too stagey . . . too much like a second-rate movie script," Ironside replied.

"What kind of a reason is that?" Ed demanded. "If I gave that to you as a reason —"

"All right, all right," Ironside broke in. "We'll consider it. We'll keep it in mind. In the meantime, however, let's concentrate on facts, not fantasy."

"In other words, we're not allowed to suspect Mr. Tuck. Is that it?" Eve asked sharply.

Ironside looked at her. "Is that what I said?"

"It's the impression I got. Whenever anybody comes up with anything that might implicate Mr. Tuck, who is practically a carbon copy of a certain Mr. Ironside —"

"Just hold it," Ironside interrupted. He called up to Mark. "Pull over," he ordered. "We're dropping off a passenger."

Ed and Eve exchanged looks.

"I broke in on you," Ironside said to Eve, "because I didn't want you to say something you might regret. I don't want you to think, though, that I'm suppressing you. Since you seem convinced that Ed's theory is correct, I'm going to let you prove it."

"I didn't mean —"

141

"Get a cab and go back to Tournabeau's hotel," Ironside went on. "Stake him out; follow him wherever he goes. If you spot him trying to peddle an armload of valuable paintings to somebody in a dark alley, you whistle for us." He looked at her evenly. "You know how to whistle, don't you?"

Eve nodded.

"We'll be expecting to hear from you," Ironside said.

Angry, but controlling her temper, Eve got out.

"Onward!" Ironside called to Mark.

"Wasn't that a little mean?" Ed asked.

Ironside smiled. "No," he replied. "It was simply an assignment. Your theory might be right. I think it would be wise to keep an eye on Tournabeau. But my way of giving the assignment was a bit more dramatic than usual, wouldn't you say?"

Ed laughed. "Decidedly."

"I sometimes go to great lengths to keep my associates happy," Ironside said.

A few minutes later the paddy wagon stopped again.

"This is it," Mark reported.

Ironside and Ed looked out. The van had halted on a steep hill. The area looked nothing at all like an artists' colony. The houses were ordinary and neat.

"This couldn't be the place," Ironside said.

"This is the address," Mark insisted.

"It's also the place," Ed said. He pointed. "Right there at street level," he said. "His name is on the window."

142

Ironside saw what looked like a shop. There was a large window. It was painted black, however, with Paul Drum's name on it in white lettering.

"It doesn't say what he sells," Ironside mused. "Maybe you're supposed to know." He shrugged. "Let's find out."

Mark got out and lowered Ironside to the street, then the three went to the door of the shop and Mark knocked. There was no answer.

Ironside reached out, turned the door handle, and pushed. The door swung open. The interior was well lighted, supplied with sunlight from large, unpainted windows at the rear. A great number of canvases — faces to the walls — were stacked at both sides of the room. At the other end there was a door, and it was open.

"That's an invitation if I ever saw one," Ironside said.

With Ironside leading the way, they entered the shop, then proceeded slowly toward the rear door.

"If these are all his," Ed said, indicating the canvases, "he sure keeps himself busy."

"Doesn't he ever sell any of them?" Mark wondered.

They passed through the rear door and entered a small but lovely garden that was separated from the rest of the world by a high surrounding wall. To the right there was an outside stairway that led upward to living quarters.

"What were you doing in there in the cemetery?" a high-pitched but definitely male voice asked.

143

Turning toward the sound, they saw a middle-aged man in the corner of the garden. He was standing in front of a canvas on an easel, and he had a brush in his hand. On a small table at his side was a square of tin with several colors of paint smeared on it.

"Did you say the cemetery?" Ironside asked, wheeling himself toward the man. "Are you Paul Drum?"

"Yes and yes," Drum replied. He was plump and peach-cheeked and was wearing a tattered gray sweatshirt and jeans that were a size or two too small. "You, of course, are the fuzz," he said. "I've read about you. You're the ex-superduper detective."

"Not 'ex' yet," Mark said.

"I'm curious about your cemetery," Ironside said. "What's buried in there?"

"Didn't you see the bodies? They're stacked against the walls. I'd bury them, but they might come back into style one of these days. If they do, I'll have myself a mint."

"Let me guess. Those are paintings of yours, but in an out-of-fashion style. Right?"

Drum nodded. "I have a painting in there of this garden that looks exactly like this garden," he said. "It's magnificent. I couldn't *give* it away. Not today, anyway. But in about . . . oh, in about fifty years, it will be worth a fortune. I won't be, though. I'll be long gone. Are you interested in investing? I'll sell you that painting cheap."

Ironside shook his head, smiling. "No, thank you."

144

He indicated the canvas. "Is that what's in style these days?"

"You're seeing the birth of a masterpiece," Drum said.

Ironside looked at the canvas more closely. "What is it? Should I know?"

"Can't you tell?"

"Not yet. I guess you haven't got far enough with it."

"I only started a few minutes ago," Drum said. "Still, you ought to be able to tell what it is." He indicated a color on the canvas. "Doesn't that blue give it away? Where else have you ever seen a blue like that?"

"I haven't the faintest idea."

"It's going to be a Rice Krispies box."

"Oh."

"That doesn't interest you, either, apparently," Drum said. "So, if you're not interested in art, why are you here? Don't tell me one of my customers is charging me with fraud again."

Ironside laughed. "Is that what happened before?"

Drum nodded. "They said I tried to pass off ordinary paintings as masterpieces. What did they expect? Every artist views his own works as masterpieces."

"How about other artists' works?" Ironside asked.

"That's not just an idle question, I assume," Drum replied. "What are you getting at?"

"You sold a number of paintings to David Tuck. Are they masterpieces?"

"According to whom?"

"Let me put it another way," Ironside said. "Are they

145

as valuable as they're claimed to be?"

"Artistically or financially?"

"Mr. Drum, shall we stop playing games? You know what I'm talking about."

"Well, I know what I got for them," Drum replied. "It wasn't very much."

"That doesn't answer the question."

"Why are you asking me?" Drum said. "Ask Halverson. He's the one who authenticated them. Do you know about him?"

"Do I know what about him?"

"Who's playing games now?" Drum smiled. "Are you aware of him, I meant. He's the one who authenticated the paintings for Tuck."

Ironside nodded. "Yes, I know about him. But I'm interested in your opinion. Were the paintings really valuable?"

Drum turned away. He put his brush into the paint on the square of tin, then daubed at the canvas. "Halverson is the expert," he replied.

"It's interesting that you got the paintings all in one batch," Ironside said.

Drum shrugged. "If you think it's interesting, then I suppose it's interesting."

"How did it happen?"

"My fairy godmother."

Ironside was silent for a second. Then he said, "We can go to Headquarters to talk about this if you want it that way."

"That won't be necessary — I hope. What was the question?"

"How did it happen that you got all those paintings at once?"

"A friend sent them to me from Europe," Drum replied. "He picked them up for practically nothing and shipped them to me. The idea was that I might be able to sell them here for a profit."

"And you did."

Drum made a disgruntled sound.

"But you're not happy," Ironside said wryly. "You said a moment ago, I think, that you didn't get much for the paintings. Weren't you aware of their value?"

"A thing like that is always a gamble," Drum said.

"How's that?"

"I saw that they'd been overpainted. I cleaned them down. They looked valuable to me. But you can never be sure about a thing like that."

"Uh-huh. Or was this the way it happened? You cleaned them down and found the originals underneath. They looked pretty good to you. But you didn't believe for a second that they were really valuable. What you actually thought was that they could be passed off as valuable. So you peddled them to David Tuck. To your considerable surprise, Tuck then had them appraised, and they turned out to be worth several million dollars — and you have been kicking yourself ever since."

Drum seemed unfazed by the story. "So that's how

147

it happened, eh?" he said. "Okay, if you say so. I never argue with the fuzz."

"I wonder," Ironside said. "Have you been doing anything about it — in addition to kicking yourself?"

Drum turned away from the canvas and looked at him. "Like what?"

"A question cannot be answered with a question."

"It was your idea. I thought you probably had some notion of what you were talking about. Evidently not."

"Have you ever been tempted to get those paintings back?" Ironside asked.

"I'm a sound sleeper; I never dream," Drum replied.

"Do you sell many of your own paintings?" Ironside asked.

"Some."

"But not many?"

Drum faced him again. "Am I a financially successful artist? No," he said. "But I enjoy painting, so I paint. Is that all right? Or is that all of a sudden against the law?"

"Perfectly legal. It might be a strain, though, if you'd acquired the habit of eating regularly. I assume that you have an income from somewhere else."

"Not exactly," Drum replied, beginning to paint again.

"This is a lovely garden," Ironside said, "and a pleasant house. But . . . uh . . . it's not the sort of setting in which I'd expect to find a simple painter of Rice Krispies boxes."

148

"It's practical," Drum said. "The price is right; it's my mother's house."

"I see."

"I'm forty-two years old, and I'm supported by my mother," Drum said. "Does that explain everything?"

"It will do," Ironside replied.

"You didn't really think I stole those paintings, did you?"

"No comment."

"I couldn't have," Drum said.

"Oh?"

Drum looked up toward the house, where, Ironside assumed, his mother was in residence. "I'm not allowed to cross the street," he said.

Ironside glanced at Ed, then at Mark, and then turned his wheelchair. "Thank you for your time," he said to Drum, and departed.

When they were in the paddy wagon again, Mark asked, "Where to?"

"Home."

The van moved forward.

"Sad," Ed said.

"I doubt that Paul Drum is as much under his mother's thumb as he'd like us to believe," Ironside said. "He didn't contact David Tuck and try to pull a fast swindle on him without crossing the street."

"Swindle? How can you say that?"

"Weren't you listening?" Ironside exclaimed. "I explained it to Drum. He thought those paintings were

149

fakes. That's why he sold them cheaply to Tuck. He thought he was making a killing."

"How did Tuck recognize them as authentic?"

"Instinct, I guess. That's how he's made it — by outsmarting people who were trying to outsmart him."

"By being a born winner," Mark said from the front seat.

"If that's true, then we're right back where we started," Ed said. "That means that the paintings are really valuable — and that Tuck again ceases to be a suspect. We should have left well enough alone."

"No, we're simply replacing him with a different suspect," Ironside said. "It wouldn't be very clever of us, would it, to accept Drum's story at face value? Maybe he is a nice little boy who's allowed to go out of the yard only occasionally to try to pull a swindle. But, on the other hand, maybe that's simply the mask he works behind. Maybe he's only a part-time painter but a full-time swindler. I'd like to know a little more about him."

"Do I smell an assignment coming up?" Ed asked.

Ironside nodded. "Go and mingle with the artists for a few days," he said. "Mention Drum's name. See if you get any bites." He looked thoughtful. "The art people have a sort of underworld all their own," he said. "When we get back to Headquarters, talk to some of the boys who've worked on stolen art cases. Find out who knows what, and where he or she can be found. I'd like to know more about Drum."

"You're assuming that he's a part of that underworld."

150

"Guessing," Ironside corrected. "He may have no connection with it at all."

"Anyway, I'm glad we're not chasing David Tuck anymore," Ed said. "I was beginning —"

"Who says we're not chasing him anymore?"

"I just assumed —"

"Tuck is still a suspect," Ironside said gruffly. "And you and Eve both can stop telling me whom I consider a suspect and whom I don't!" He called up to Mark. "Can't this crate move any faster? Ed has work to do, and he's anxious to get at it!"

9 The Real Thing!

IRONSIDE WAS like a bear with a sore paw during the next few days. Scowling, he wheeled himself about his quarters, his shoulders hunched, like an animal looking for something to sink its teeth into. He received regular reports from Eve, who was watching Harry Tournabeau, and from Ed, who was probing for information in the art underworld, but they had nothing to tell him that moved the case any closer to a solution. He was still baffled by the how of it, and it looked as if the explanation might elude him forever.

152

"Think of something!" Ironside snapped at Mark.

"Spinach with chocolate sauce."

"You know what I mean. Tell me any possible way that those paintings could have been taken off that truck. I don't care how wild it is. I'm ready to believe almost anything."

"The thief followed the truck with a big vacuum cleaner and sucked the paintings out of the crates. Wild enough?"

Ironside did not answer. He rolled his chair to a window and sat there sulking.

"I told you I didn't get anything out of Jones," Mark said, "so I don't know anything you don't. If you can't figure it out, how do you expect me to?"

"We know the paintings went onto the truck," Ironside said.

"Right."

"We have no evidence to suggest that a stop was made along the way."

"Right."

"But the paintings were not in the crates when the truck arrived at the auction house."

"Right."

"Wait a minute. Let's go back to the beginning. How do we know that the paintings went onto the truck?"

"Tuck said so, Jones said so, Buckley said so. Do you think they were all lying?"

"Maybe Tuck only assumes that they were put on the truck," Ironside said. "He saw Jones and Buckley take the crates from the room, but he *didn't* actually see them put them on the truck. He stayed in the room, remember? He was still overseeing the job. And he didn't observe them from the window. I asked about that, and he specifically said that he had *not* looked out the window."

"Okay. What happened?" Mark asked.

Ironside faced the window again, looking out, saying nothing for a moment. "They took the crates —" he sighed deeply — "took the crates where? Did they stash them in another room along the way?"

"Hold it," Mark said. "They had the crates on the truck when they got back to the auction house. It was only the paintings that were missing."

Ironside nodded. "They could have had those empty crates in the truck when they arrived. This wasn't a spur-of-the-moment thing. Let's say it happened this way: They arrived with the truck full of empty crates. They went through the routine — the packing, the signing, the carrying out. But instead of taking the crated paintings to the truck, they dropped them . . . where? Another room? That's the only logical place I can think of at the moment. Anyway, they dropped them someplace. Then they got into the truck and drove to the auction house — and were aghast to discover, upon their arrival, that they had empty crates in the truck. How does that sound?"

"I like it," Mark replied. "It'll make a great movie. But who'll play the truck?"

154

"Will you stop it? It could have been done that way, couldn't it?"

Mark nodded. "Right. So where are the paintings now? Still in that room?"

"Obviously that's an important question." Ironside hedged.

"Do you want me to repeat it?"

"No." He wheeled himself toward the exit. "I want to look in those rooms," he said. "Let's go to visit our friend Tuck again."

Ironside and Mark drove to the Tuck estate. Tuck, not having been told that they were coming, was not present. They were immediately admitted to the castle grounds, however, and, a few minutes later, to the castle itself.

When they reached Tuck's office, Ironside explained to Mrs. Alcorn what he wanted.

"Just to look around?" she asked, puzzled.

"Yes, I suppose you could say that."

"Well . . . I really. . . ."

"Contact Mr. Tuck," Ironside suggested. "As a matter of fact, I think you should. Tell him I want to make a thorough search."

"That *would* be best," Mrs. Alcorn said.

She put in the call to Tuck, who was at his office in the city, and told him what Ironside wanted to do. Tuck's response was immediate.

"He said to tell you to enjoy yourself," Mrs. Alcorn reported.

155

Ironside grunted, then wheeled himself away, followed by Mark, to begin the search.

"He sure wasn't worried about what you might find," Mark commented.

"Well . . . he couldn't have stopped me. I could have gotten a warrant."

"It would have taken time. If he'd wanted to hide anything, his best move would have been to make you get the warrant."

Ironside grunted again. "We'll see."

They went from room to room along the corridors of the lower floors. They discovered that the rooms looked a great deal alike, but, other than that, they found nothing that particularly interested them.

"That doesn't prove that my theory isn't right," Ironside contended. "They could have stashed the crates in one of these rooms, then removed them later."

"How? How would they get in here? There's a guard with a shotgun at the gate, and the place is fenced in."

"Tournabeau got in without going through the gate," Ironside said.

"Yes, but Tournabeau had spent a lot of time here, and he knows the security setup. Buckley and — Oh, yes . . . I see what you mean. That puts Tournabeau right back in the middle of it, doesn't it?"

"It's possible," Ironside said. "They could have put the paintings in one of the rooms, then, with Tournabeau telling them how, slipped in here later and taken them out. This is a big place, this castle. An army could be

156

in here marching around, and no one would know it."

"Then Tournabeau is calling the signals?" Mark asked.

"As I said, it's possible. I'm just trying to figure out how it could have been managed. And this way, to me, makes sense."

Mark nodded. "It's making sense, all right. What now?"

"Back to Headquarters. The next step is to figure out where the paintings went from here, and then to track them down."

On the way back to the city, Ironside had a call from Eve.

"We're saving a dime," she told Ironside. "I'm reporting not only for myself, but for Ed, too."

"I suppose there's an explanation that goes with that," Ironside replied gruffly.

"You told me to follow Tournabeau, and I'm following him. Right now he's in the flea market, which also happens to be the section where members of the art underworld hang out. Get the connection?"

"Yes," Ironside replied eagerly. "Who spotted whom? Did Ed spot you, or did you spot Ed?"

"We made a pact not to reveal that information," Eve answered mysteriously.

"I see. Is there anything you *can* reveal?"

"I can tell you what Tournabeau is doing. He's wandering from store —" Eve stopped. "Maybe store isn't the right term. They're little hole-in-the-wall places that

158

sell cheap paintings. Anyway, he's wandering from place
to place asking questions. Ed has been keeping close to
him, listening. We switched assignments temporarily.
Ed thought he might be more likely to see me and
realize that he's being tailed."

"Logical. What kind of questions?"

"Ed hasn't been able to get close enough to hear
many of them," Eve told him. "But it's obvious that
the people he's talking to are explaining things to him."

"All right. Stay with it, both of you. And let me know
if he seems to be trying to make a deal with somebody."

Ironside hung up, then told Mark what Eve had said.

"It fits in," Mark said. "It looks as if your guess was
right. Tournabeau is stage-managing the whole deal."

"I don't know," Ironside said, troubled. "My impression now is just the opposite."

"The opposite? What's Tournabeau doing down there
at the flea market if he isn't trying to sell paintings?"

"You met Tournabeau," Ironside said. "Did he strike
you as the type who would steal several million dollars'
worth of paintings and *then* try to figure out what to
do with them?"

"No."

"Of course not. I imagine Tournabeau knows exactly
what he's doing every second of every waking hour. He's
definitely not the sort who goes from door to door trying
to peddle stolen paintings."

"Door to door?"

"All right . . . shop to shop. My point is this: If

159

Tournabeau intended to put the grab on those paintings, he'd have a buyer for them lined up before he did it."

"What's he doing at the flea market, then?"

"What was Ed doing?"

"Trying to get a lead."

"All right, maybe that's what Tournabeau is doing, too. Don't forget — we decided before that Tournabeau really thinks those paintings are fakes and that Tuck arranged for them to be stolen. Tournabeau might be down there in the flea market trying to get information that would link Tuck to the theft."

"Detective work, eh?"

"It's possible. I find it extremely difficult to believe that a man like Tournabeau would walk around in the open trying to peddle hot merchandise."

"He didn't seem that dumb," Mark agreed. "But what about your theory that the paintings were stashed in another room, and that Tournabeau showed Buckley and Jones how to get back into the grounds to move them out?"

"I'm not discarding it. I'm just —" he sighed gloomily — "just not as happy with it as I was at first."

"Doesn't a lot of this depend on whether those paintings are real or fake?" Mark asked.

"I don't think there's really much doubt that they're real."

"Halverson didn't exactly say, did he?" Mark said.

Ironside frowned. "Sure he did. At least he — If he

160

didn't say it, he implied it."

"Saying it is one thing and —"

"All right. Let's go to see Halverson again."

They soon reached the city, and Mark drove straight to the art gallery. When they entered there was no one in sight, as before. But a few seconds later a young man appeared from the rear of the gallery. This time, however, he turned back as soon as he saw them.

"What does that mean?" Mark asked. "Yankee go home?"

"I suppose we'll find out."

Not long after that the elder Halverson emerged from the rooms behind the gallery. He stopped for a moment, peered in the direction of his visitors, then approached them. The first time they had seen the small, dumpy-looking man, he had been smiling cordially. That cordiality had quickly vanished, however. Now he was looking somewhat contrite.

"Chief Ironside, I must apologize. . . ."

"I accept. What did you do?"

"I acted in a terrible manner when you were here before. But I was . . . I was annoyed. Not at you, understand. I was angry at myself."

"So you took it out on me?"

"Yes." He gestured toward the rear. "Will you come to my office? It will be more comfortable there."

"All right . . . thank you."

Alver Halverson led the way to the back of the gallery, through a fairly narrow doorway, and then along

161

a short corridor that was lined with empty frames. He halted at another doorway and ushered Ironside and Mark into his office. The room was cluttered with frames and files and rolls of canvas.

"Perhaps not more comfortable," Halverson said, clearing off a chair so that Mark could sit down, "but more private. I have a confession to make."

Ironside and Mark exchanged looks.

Halverson gestured toward the chair, inviting Mark to be seated. He moved to his own large rolltop desk and settled in his swivel chair.

"I am guilty," he said glumly. "I do not know — perhaps it may even be a matter for the police."

Ironside studied him closely. "Guilty of what?"

"It's the paintings — the paintings owned by Mr. David Tuck."

Ironside looked disappointed. "I suspected everybody but you," he said.

Halverson made a nervous, drumming sound with his fingers on his desk. "This is difficult," he said. "I do not know exactly how to explain it. I asked my son, and he told me that I was wrong not to have revealed it to you. But, now that I have made up my mind to tell you, it is difficult. . . ."

"You could start at the beginning," Ironside said. "That's the conventional way."

"Yes, that would be best. It is necessary to understand all of it, not just a part of it. Well, it began when Mr. Tuck came to me and told me that he had these

162

paintings that he wanted evaluated. At first I did not even want to see him. But my son —"

"Just a minute," Ironside broke in. "Why didn't you want to see him?"

"I have no liking for people like Mr. Tuck."

"I don't understand. What makes him an undesirable?"

"He uses art to make money. That is his only interest in it. When he looks at a Picasso, a Manet, a Vuillard, what does he see? A painting? No! He sees money."

Ironside nodded. "All right, go on."

"As I say, I did not want to see him. But my son said that I should, so I did."

"And he told you that he had a number of paintings that he wanted evaluated. Right?"

"Yes. He explained that he had gotten hold of them through a stroke of luck. He said he was sure that they were worth several millions of dollars. Then he said to me that he would pay me a certain fee to look at the paintings and tell him if his judgment was correct." Halverson lowered his gaze. "This amount of money that he mentioned to me was many times greater than the fee I usually receive."

"How did he explain that?"

"He did not explain it. It was not necessary to explain it. He offered me this great amount of money before I even told him what my fee would be. The implication was quite clear."

"All right, tell me what he meant," Ironside said.

163

"He wanted to buy me — just as he would buy a Picasso or a Vuillard."

"Did he say that?"

"He did not have to say it. I knew what he wanted. He had these paintings, which he was certain were not authentic, and he wanted me to authenticate them and make them worth several millions of dollars."

Ironside leaned forward. "The paintings, then, were fakes?"

Halverson looked up, frowning. "No, no."

"You just said —"

"I said only that Mr. Tuck thought they were, as you say, fakes."

Ironside leaned back. "Okay, go on with the story."

"So I said yes, I would evaluate the paintings. I did not say how much the fee would be, though. I was angry; I had been insulted. I did not even want to speak to the man again."

"Then I don't understand why you agreed to evaluate the paintings."

"Should the paintings suffer because they were purchased by a man like Mr. Tuck? No. They deserved to be judged, so I agreed to do it. I assumed, of course, that they would prove to be copies . . . very poorly done. And that is what I would tell Mr. Tuck. But I was wrong. Oh, they were authentic, all right. Fantastic! Marvelous! Great paintings!"

"And that is what you told Mr. Tuck?"

"Naturally."

164

Ironside leaned forward again, looking puzzled this time. "What are you guilty of?"

"I have not finished the story."

"Please go on."

"Soon I received a check from Mr. Tuck. It was for the amount he had mentioned . . . much, much more than my accustomed fee. I realized immediately, of course, what had happened. He thought that he had been able to buy me." Once more he lowered his eyes. "To this day, Chief Ironside, I have not told him the truth. I kept the money, and I allowed him to think that he had been very clever. Do you see? It was my revenge. I was repaying him for thinking that he could buy me. He had not been clever at all. He had simply paid a great deal of money for something that he could have had for a lot less. I thought it was amusing."

Ironside regarded him unsmilingly.

Halverson sighed. "My son did not see the humor of it, either," he said. "He decided that I should tell you what I had done. I am ready to accept the punishment."

Ironside shook his head. "Punishment for what?"

"I have deceived a client. I overcharged him."

Ironside and Mark looked at each other again.

"Should I call my lawyer?" Halverson asked.

Ironside shook his head again. "I don't really think that will be necessary," he replied. "Mr. Halverson, I — Well, frankly, I'm afraid you'll have to work out that problem on your own. Unless you're guilty of something a little more serious than overcharging Mr. Tuck, I just

165

don't think I can be of much help to you. I thought. . . .
I guess it isn't important what I thought."

"What was it?" Halverson asked, curious.

"I thought you were going to tell me that you were
involved in the stealing of the paintings."

Halverson drew himself up. "That is preposterous!"
Ironside laughed. "Yes, I guess it is," he agreed.

"Why would I steal the paintings?" Halverson continued. "Paintings that are stolen must be kept hidden.
I would not do that to a painting. A painting needs to
be hung and seen and enjoyed."

"I'll take your word for it," Ironside replied. "Answer this for me, though. And it's extremely important.
Is there any possibility — any possibility at all — that
those paintings were not authentic?"

Halverson shook his head emphatically. "Absolutely
none. I staked my reputation on it when I informed
Mr. Tuck that they were genuine."

"All right, thank you, thank you again," Ironside said.

He and Mark left the gallery, boarded the paddy
wagon, and headed for Headquarters.

"Well, that seems to let Halverson out, but it puts
Tuck right back in," Mark said.

"How do you figure that?"

"According to Halverson, Tuck thought those paintings were fakes. So he didn't dare put them up for sale
at the auction. The only way he could turn them into
money — big money — was to have them stolen and
collect the insurance."

166

"Very neat."

"But you don't think it happened that way?"

"What evidence do we have that Tuck thought they were fakes?"

"Halverson said so — plus the price Tuck paid for having them authenticated."

"According to Halverson," Ironside said, "Tuck was being cute, trying to 'buy him.' But how does he know that? Did Tuck actually tell him that he thought the paintings were fakes? No. All he did was to offer him a larger fee than Halverson was used to getting. Now, does that prove that Tuck looked on the paintings as fakes?"

"Not exactly. . . ."

"No. Isn't it just possible that all this melodrama — Tuck trying to 'buy' Halverson, Tuck really thinking the paintings were fakes, Halverson responding to cunning with cunning — happened nowhere but in Halverson's imagination? An emotional element was present, you know. Halverson disliked — still dislikes — Tuck very much."

"Yes, I guess so," Mark sighed.

"We have no way of knowing what, exactly, Tuck was paying for. Maybe it *was* an attempt to 'buy' Halverson. Or maybe he just wanted good and fast service. Or maybe, by overpaying, he was trying to impress a man who clearly didn't like him. I don't know. And I don't think we can find out by asking Tuck. How could we be sure that his answer would be the truth. No, for the time being we're stuck with Halverson's story, and I think we ought to take it with a very large grain of salt."

When they reached Headquarters they found Eve there. She was slumped in a chair, sound asleep.

"What is this?" Ironside roared. "What am I running, a flophouse?"

The thunder awakened Eve. She sat up, blinking and looking around, wondering where the sound had come from.

"First, Ed; now, you," Ironside said. "What do I have working for me, a pair of sleeping beauties?"

Eve yawned. "I deserve a little rest. Do you realize how long I've been keeping tabs on Harry Tournabeau?"

"Don't tell me," Ironside replied. "Since you're not paid overtime, you'd be wasting your breath."

"If he gets a rest, why don't I?"

"How do you know he's resting?"

"He went back to his suite and left a call for eight tonight — in time for dinner, I assume. So I thought I'd take advantage of the opportunity and try to get a little rest myself."

"Why here?"

"I thought I'd better report in first."

"Good thinking," Ironside said. He gestured. "Go back to sleep," he said. "We'll call you when it's time to pick up Tournabeau's trail again."

"I've sort of lost the desire," Eve said, rising. She turned to Mark. "Is there anything around to snack on?"

He waved in the general direction of the kitchen. "Be my guest."

Eve disappeared, and returned a few minutes later munching on a sesame seed cracker. "Do you know anything I don't know?" she asked Ironside.

He looked at her scathingly.

"About the case, I mean," she said.

Ironside told her about his talk with Alver Halverson.

"But you decided in favor of Tuck again, apparently," she said when he had finished.

"Watch it, young lady, or you'll find yourself back in the lobby of Tournabeau's hotel."

"Admit it, though," she said. "Don't you always find some way to shift the blame away from Tuck?"

"Eve, I think things out. If I find Tuck in the role of the victim instead of the perpetrator, that's just the way the facts happen to fall."

"Well, I suppose you've convinced yourself that —"

"Don't say it!" Ironside warned.

Cowed, Eve nodded and returned to the chair she had vacated.

A few moments later Ed arrived. He dropped wearily into another chair.

"Well, it may not have been a productive day," Ironside said, "but, from appearances, it's certainly been a busy one."

"I might as well be out pounding a beat, the punishment my feet are getting," Ed complained.

"What did you find out, if anything?"

169

"I found a number of places where I could get a genuine Rembrandt for a couple hundred bucks — or fifty bucks, if that was all I happened to have on me."

"Sounds like a good deal," Ironside said. "On the open market you could probably turn around and get a cool five hundred for a genuine Rembrandt."

Eve sat up. "What do you mean? You could get closer to a million dollars for — Oh, sorry. I didn't know this was the comedy hour."

"I take it you didn't find out anything we could use," Ironside said to Ed.

Ed shook his head. "I wish I knew what Tournabeau found out, though," he said. "I just couldn't get close enough to him."

"How did he look when he left?" Ironside asked. "Sad? Glad?"

Ed turned to Eve. "What would you say?"

"You probably got a better look at him than I did."

"But you followed him. How did he look *after* he left?"

"That wasn't my question," Ironside interjected.

"If I had to describe it, I suppose I'd say he looked . . . well . . . satisfied," Ed said.

Eve nodded agreement. "Satisfied — that's exactly the word."

"That's why I wish I knew what he found out," Ed said. "It may have been something we'd like to know, too. That is, if Tournabeau is competing with us to break this case."

"You should have asked," Ironside said.

170

"Asked him?"

"No, no. You should have talked to some of the same people he talked to. You should have found out what he was asking them."

"They'd have known I was a cop."

"So?"

"You know how fast the word travels in an area like that," Ed replied. "I wouldn't have been able to finish the job you sent me to do."

"Yes, I suppose you're right," Ironside said slowly. "Do you remember who Tournabeau was talking to?"

"I don't have the names," Ed answered. "But I made notes. I have the locations and descriptions."

"Then that's our mission for tomorrow," Ironside said. "We'll question the same people — if we can find them. Maybe by this time tomorrow, if we're lucky, we'll know what Tournabeau knows."

Neither Ed nor Eve offered any comment. It was clear to them that, considering Ironside's mood, silence was indicated.

10 Cover-up Uncovered

IRONSIDE AND MARK left for the flea market alone the next morning. Eve had picked up Tournabeau's trail the evening before and had followed him during most of the night. She was now trying to catch up on her sleep. Ed, meanwhile, had taken her place as Tournabeau's shadow. He was at present stationed in the lobby of the hotel, waiting for Tournabeau to begin the day.

Reaching the flea market, Ironside proceeded to seek out shopkeepers who fitted the descriptions that Ed had compiled. He met with no difficulty. The descriptions were detailed, so that it was easy to spot the dealers. And the dealers, once Ironside had identified himself, were in no way reluctant to talk about Tournabeau. It was obvious that he was a stranger to them. It was clear, also, that he had not been offering to sell them paintings. He had simply been making conversation and then cleverly working David Tuck's name into the talk.

What surprised Ironside and Mark was that the dealers were so well acquainted with Tuck, not just as a name in the newspapers, but as a customer. It seemed that he quite often purchased paintings in large quantities and then had them shipped to out-of-town factories, where, the dealers assumed, they were used in decorating offices.

Shortly after noon, after having talked to nearly a dozen dealers, Ironside and Mark got back into the van and drove toward Headquarters. A few moments later the phone rang. It was Ed Brown calling.

"I've been trying to get you all morning," Ed said. "What happened?" His voice was excited.

"Nothing," Ironside replied. "We were talking to your friends, the art dealers. Very interesting."

"I don't know what you learned, but it couldn't be much more interesting than this. Harry Tournabeau is back at the Tuck castle."

"How did he get in?" Ironside asked quickly.

"Through the front gate. I was watching from a distance away, but it looked as if he were expected. He must have called Tuck first."

173

"How long has he been there?" Ironside asked, checking his watch.

"Most of the morning. He went directly from the hotel. Chief, it isn't just a casual visit. He was carrying a couple of attaché cases. I think he's working for Tuck again."

"That's very doubtful. Tuck didn't strike me as the type who could forgive and forget that quickly."

"Shall I sit it out?" Ed asked.

"No. Come back to Headquarters. Mark and I are on our way there now. I'll tell you what I discovered at the market, and we can discuss this new wrinkle — Tournabeau and Tuck."

When Ironside and Mark reached Headquarters, Eve was there. Mark went to the kitchen to prepare lunch.

"Are you fresh and alert of mind?" Ironside asked Eve. "If you are, tell me why David Tuck would take Tournabeau back under his wing."

"Only as a last resort. That would be my guess," she replied. "Did he?"

"We don't know." He told her what Ed had learned and what he had surmised from it.

Before long, Ed arrived. A few minutes later Mark produced lunch and the four sat down around the table. Ed asked what Ironside had found out at the flea market.

"Tuck buys paintings by the . . . well, not quite by the carload, but almost. And he made his most recent purchase only a few weeks ago."

"From one dealer or many?" Ed asked.

"From many. He buys them, the dealers say, for his

174

companies. The paintings are used in decorating the offices."

"That sounds logical," Eve said.

"Why does Tuck do the buying?" Ed asked. "Doesn't he have a professional decorator working for him? Why wouldn't the pro do the buying?"

"Well, Tuck likes to take care of all the details himself," Ironside replied. "But it isn't the fact that he did the buying personally that interests me so much. The fascinating aspect of it is that he was so specific and careful in doing the buying. I learned from the dealers that this last time he bought pictures of a certain size."

"*What* size?" Eve asked.

"Various sizes. But, the point is, he knew exactly what sizes he was looking for, and he bought paintings that were as close to that size as possible. Why?"

"Were these paintings for offices?" Ed asked.

"I have no idea," Ironside replied. "All I know is that he bought them and that he looked for specific sizes."

"How many?" Eve asked.

Ironside thought for a moment, then replied, "Fifty or sixty, probably. That's only a rough guess."

"He took fifty-seven paintings off the walls," Eve said. "Maybe he bought these to replace the ones that came down."

Ironside nodded. "That sounds right. He told us he bought cheap paintings to hang in place of the ones he planned to sell. But why did he buy them —" He nodded

175

again. "Yes, I think I see. . . ."

"Of course," Eve said. "When you take a painting down, there's a clean place behind it. In an old castle like that, I guess it would be especially obvious. He wanted paintings to fill up the spaces exactly."

"Did he have to get that close to it?" Ed asked. "Larger paintings would have accomplished the same thing."

"That's true," Ironside agreed. "But simply covering up probably wouldn't have suited Tuck. He'd probably want to fill those vacant spaces as perfectly as possible. Some people are bugs on perfection."

"Well, that answers that question and gets us exactly nowhere," Eve said. "We don't know any more now than we did before."

"Let's leave that for a while and see if we can figure out why Tuck would take Tournabeau back into the castle," Ironside said. "I find it very difficult to believe."

"I don't know that he's back there," Ed said. "All I can say for sure is that Tournabeau went in without any trouble, took a couple of attaché cases in with him, and didn't come back out. At least he hadn't when I left."

"Maybe it was a settling up of affairs," Eve suggested.

"And maybe it wasn't," Ironside said. "A couple of days ago Tournabeau slipped into the castle and stole some papers from Tuck's private file, and Tuck took a few shots at him. Does it make sense that today they'd be on even a conversation basis?"

176

She shook her head.

"Let's not be too sure about that," Ed said. "If Tuck is in trouble with his businesses, maybe he needs Tournabeau's help — as his right-hand man, I mean. When you get used to operating with an assistant you can trust, you —" Suddenly he decided he did not like his own theory. "No, he couldn't trust him anymore, could he?"

"It does not fit," Ironside said crossly. "It is not like Tuck to take Tournabeau back. My guess is that this hasn't happened."

"Then what's Tournabeau doing at the castle?"

"Getting some personal belongings."

"And it's taking him all morning?" Ed asked.

"All right, let's find out," Ironside said. "We have an excuse for going to the castle. We're still working on this case. Let's drive out there and see what strange thing is going on. Mark! Get the bus!"

On the way to the Tuck estate, Ironside decided it might be wise to telephone and inform Tuck that he, Eve, Ed, and Mark were on the way. Eve made the call.

"His secretary says he isn't there," she reported to Ironside, holding a hand over the mouthpiece. "They left for the city about an hour ago. Tournabeau was with him."

Ironside grunted.

"What shall I tell her?"

"Tell her . . . tell her we'll be along in a few minutes, anyway. Tell her to clear us at the gate. Tell her it's with regard to the case."

177

Eve passed along the message, then hung up.

"How did she take it?" Ironside asked.

"In stride. She seems to have the idea that, as far as Tuck is concerned, you have the run of the castle. She said that if you wanted her for anything, just to let her know."

"Good. That'll give us a chance to look around at our leisure."

They reached the gate to the grounds not long after that and were waved on through. When they reached the castle they were met by the middle-aged man who acted as the general caretaker. He offered to assist them. Ironside thanked him but told him he would not be needed, and the man disappeared into the depths of the castle.

"Let's look at the floor where the paintings were crated," Ironside said, wheeling himself toward the elevator. "We examined the rooms on the other floors, but we skipped that one."

"Why?" Ed asked.

"Why did we skip it? We were working on the theory that Buckley and Jones had dropped the paintings off on a lower floor and picked them up later. We assumed they'd be doing this without Tuck's knowledge. So they would hardly use a room that was on the same floor he was on, would they?"

"Makes sense," Ed nodded.

As the door slid shut and the elevator began to rise, Eve asked, "Why would we be interested in the rooms

178

on the floor where the paintings were crated?"

"Why not?" Ironside replied. "Maybe we'll find another solution to this case. We have only about a dozen so far."

"When do we narrow it down to one?" Mark asked.

Ironside looked up at him. "Smile when you say that."

The car stopped, the door opened, and they got out. They moved along the corridor toward the room in which the paintings had been packed for transfer to the auction house. Ironside set the pace, wheeling himself slowly as he looked at the paintings on the walls.

"Some of these are probably the ones Tuck purchased from those dealers we talked to," Ironside said. "They're worth five or ten dollars apiece. Can you tell them from the valuable ones?"

"How do we know there are valuable paintings here?" Eve asked.

"That's a point. We don't. To me they all look to be of equal value. They could be worth a million or five." He shrugged. "I suppose it isn't important, unless you owned them and intended to sell them."

"Here's the room," Mark said, pointing to his left.

"No, it's the next one," Ironside said.

Mark opened the door of the room he had indicated. "This looks like it to me."

Ironside had moved on to the next door. He opened it. "You're wrong. This is it," he said. "The leftover lumber and packing material are still here."

Ironside wheeled himself into the room, and the others

179

followed, peering around curiously.

"Here's a question," Ironside mused. "Why hasn't this debris been cleared out of here? The paintings are gone; why haven't the lumber and insulating material been carted away?"

"Why haven't I cleaned out my hall closet?" Eve asked.

"Because you're too busy. But the castle has a caretaker — and people on the staff who clear out debris, presumably. So the question stands."

"Oversight," Ed guessed.

"Maybe."

"As a marker?" Mark suggested. "This way you know for sure which room the paintings were crated in. Otherwise you might think it was the room next door."

Ironside shook his head. "Tuck knows one room from the other," he said. "Jones made the same mistake you did. He went to that other room when we were here before. But Tuck knew exactly which room was which."

"Did you find any secret panels," Ed asked, looking around, "when you inspected in here before?"

"No, why?"

"Castles . . . secret panels . . . they go together."

"Let's move on," Ironside said. "I've seen enough of this room to know it like an old friend — and to be positive it has no secret panels."

They went back to the room in which Mark thought the paintings had been crated. It was completely empty. Otherwise, however, it looked exactly like the first room.

180

"They had a lot of imagination in those days," Mark commented.

"These were probably bedrooms," Ironside speculated. "For servants, perhaps." He wheeled to the window and looked out. "Same view."

"Why does the view interest you so much?" Mark asked.

"How often do I get to look out a castle window?"

As they started to leave, Ironside stopped his chair, then bent down and picked up something from the floor. But he immediately tossed it aside.

"What?" Ed asked.

"Dust puff," Ironside replied. "Even a castle gets dusty." He wheeled himself to the doorway, then halted again and examined the frame of the opening. A chip had been knocked out of the wood recently. "The caretaker doesn't take care," he said. "That ought to be repaired."

"A hundred lashes for the caretaker," Mark said.

They continued to go from room to room. The only thing they found was that all of the rooms were practically identical. The differences were so minor that they had to be looked for to be noticed.

The elevator was waiting for them when they completed the search. They started to board the car, but suddenly Ironside stopped. He wheeled himself to the painting nearest the elevator and looked at it closely.

"It isn't signed," he said after a moment.

"It's one of the cheap ones, then," Ed commented.

181

Ironside began wheeling himself along the corridor again. The others, puzzled, followed him. Several yards farther on, he stopped again. Then, after examining that painting, he said, "Here's another one — no signature."

"What's so mysterious about that?" Eve asked.

"Painters who don't sign their work?"

"But these are cheap, almost valueless paintings."

Ironside scowled. "Still. . . ."

He examined the rest of the paintings on the floor, but he found no more that were not signed. When he and the others returned to the elevator, however, the car was gone. Ed punched the button.

After a second the car appeared. When the door opened they found Mrs. Alcorn, David Tuck's secretary, inside.

"I was looking for you." She smiled. "I told Mr. Tuck you were here, and he asked me to see if I could help in any way."

"Is he back?" Ironside asked.

"No. I telephoned him."

"Oh." Ironside shook his head. "No, I don't think we need you. But thank you, anyway," he said. "We've finished. We were just leaving."

"I'll go to the door with you."

When they were all aboard the car, Mark punched the down button, and the car began to descend.

"I understand that Mr. Tournabeau is back working for Mr. Tuck," Ironside said to Mrs. Alcorn.

"Yes," she replied matter-of-factly.

"Wasn't there —"

"You'll have to discuss that with Mr. Tuck," she broke in. "I'd rather not talk about his personal relationships with other employees."

"Of course." Ironside nodded. "This is a police matter, though."

She looked at him, puzzled. "The fact that Mr. Tournabeau is working for Mr. Tuck again?"

"When we're working on a case, we assume that everything is important."

"Well, all I can tell you is that Mr. Tournabeau is back at work."

The car reached the main floor. Ironside led the way out, followed closely by Mrs. Alcorn.

"Are they buddy-buddy again?" Ironside asked.

"I don't think Mr. Tuck and Mr. Tournabeau were ever buddy-buddy," she replied. "They've always been very businesslike in their relationship."

"I see."

The caretaker was at the exit. He was inspecting a crack that had appeared in one of the stones in the floor.

"You probably don't realize it," Ironside said to him, "but you haven't had that room where the paintings were crated cleaned up yet."

"Mr. Tuck told me not to touch that room, sir," he replied.

"Did he say why?"

"Oh, yes. He said the police would want it to remain as it was."

183

"Very thoughtful of him," Ironside said, moving on.

Mrs. Alcorn waited until they were all aboard the van, then she went back into the castle. As she departed Ironside commented on the staunchness of her loyalty to David Tuck.

"A man whose associates like him. Whom does that sound like?" Eve smiled.

"Whom?" Ironside asked.

"Never mind. I'm not supposed to point out the similarity between you and Tuck anymore."

Ironside snorted. "Let's go," he said to Mark.

As they headed back toward the city, Ironside said, "That proves how unwise it is to jump to conclusions. I thought Tuck might have had some ulterior motive for leaving that room untouched. Actually, he was just trying to be helpful."

"Imagine what we'd have thought if he had hurried to get it cleaned up," Ed said. "We'd have suspected him of trying to get rid of some sort of evidence."

"On the other hand, though," Eve said, "maybe he did get rid of some sort of evidence and then left the room like that to throw us off the trail."

Ironside looked at her steadily for a moment, then, turning his chair, faced away from her. He said nothing more during the drive to Headquarters.

It was late afternoon when they arrived. Ironside wheeled himself straight to a window and stationed himself there, remaining silent, staring into space.

Ed and Eve settled down in chairs, looking glum. It

184

was clear that Ironside was not happy with the way things were going. As he had said, they had turned up a dozen solutions to the case, but the single and correct solution so far had eluded them.

"I guess I'd better do something about dinner," Mark said after a while.

"I'll help you," Eve volunteered.

"Maybe I can do something, too," Ed said.

When they all reached the kitchen Mark laughed and said, "I don't remember ever having so much willing help before. What's the matter? Afraid the Chief's gloom is catching?"

"Mark is right," Eve said to Ed. "We ought to be back in there helping the Chief."

"Helping how? I don't know the answer. And, at the moment, he obviously doesn't want to talk about it."

"He's stymied," Mark said. "I've seen him stopped before, but never like this."

"There are just too many leads — all of them good," Ed said. "We track one down, and it leaves us with two more to track down, both of them as good as the first one. How long can this go on?"

"It has to end sometime," Eve said. "When it does, maybe it'll begin to make sense."

"I'm going in," Ed said, leaving to rejoin Ironside.

Mark and Eve prepared dinner. It was ready in an hour, and they took it into the main room. Ed, who had been doing nothing but sitting, joined them at the table. Ironside, however, showed no sign that he had

185

heard dinner announced. He simply continued to sit, unmoving, his shoulders hunched, his expression set in a deep scowl.

"Good," Ed said, tasting the food. He addressed Mark. "You ought to have Eve tell you how she makes this."

Mark leaned forward, glaring. "*I* made it."

Ed raised a hand in a gesture of apology. "Peace!"

"Maybe we ought to be quiet," Eve said, nodding in Ironside's direction.

"Why?" Mark asked. "You could fire off The Bomb in here and he'd never know it."

"Shhhh. . . ." Eve cautioned. "He hears everything."

"So what? It's *Chief* Ironside, not *King* Ironside," Mark said. "We're not required to keep absolute silence while the king broods."

"A man's home is his castle," Eve said.

"Not unless the man's name is David Tuck."

"The Chief should have stayed at the castle," Mark said. "He could have had plenty of privacy there. It'd be easy enough to get lost — permanently. That place is like a maze."

"It might be fun, though, to —" Eve began.

"That's it!" Ironside suddenly thundered.

The others all turned toward him, puzzled.

"Like a maze!" Ironside said, grinning and wheeling himself toward the table. "The castle is like a maze! What happens in a maze? You get lost! You're never sure where you are, unless you happen to live in the maze and you're familiar with it."

186

"I guess you're trying to tell us something," Eve responded. "But what?"

"Think about it!"

Ironside wheeled past them and moved on to the telephone table, picked up the receiver, and dialed. "This is Gerard Mehl's number, right here beside his name on the pad, isn't it?" he said to Eve.

"I think so. Is he the one who did it?"

Ironside did not reply. By then he had Gerard Mehl on the phone. He asked him — to the puzzlement of Ed, Eve, and Mark, who were listening — about the padding that was used to pack the paintings. Mehl's reply apparently pleased Ironside, for his smile broadened. Then he asked Mehl to put Frank Buckley on the phone. He was told, apparently, that Buckley was not there, for a moment later he hung up.

"What's the packing made of?" Ed asked.

"Cotton." Ironside was dialing again.

"Hey! No wonder you were so pleased!" Mark said sarcastically.

"Keep thinking," Ironside said. "It'll mean something to you if you —" He broke in on himself. He had Frank Buckley's hotel on the phone.

Ironside had Buckley tell him again how he and Jones had transported the crates from the room down to the truck. He was not pleased with the result. He urged Buckley to try to recall anything out of the ordinary that had occurred. Buckley apparently could remember nothing that he would class as unusual. Ironside

187

asked him if there had been any accidents or minor mishaps. Buckley — if Ironside's expression was any indication — answered in the negative. Ironside then asked him to repeat the information he had provided about moving the paintings from the room to the truck once more. While Buckley complied with the request, Ironside sat listening patiently. Then, abruptly, he brightened. Yes, that was what he wanted to know, he told Buckley. He thanked him and hung up.

"Add this to what you already know," Ironside said, wheeling himself toward the table where Ed, Eve, and Mark were still seated. "There was a minor mishap while the crates were being transferred. Jones hit a doorframe with one of them."

"We saw that there was a chip out of the door," Eve said. "So?"

"But which door?" Ironside urged.

"Out of —" She shrugged. "I can't remember. Out of the frame of the door to the room the paintings were packed in, I think."

"No. It was the room next door," Mark said.

"Right!"

Ironside was wheeling himself back to the phone. "What have you got on that information about the cotton?" he asked.

"You're going too fast," Eve complained.

"I'm rolling. I can't stop when I'm rolling." He picked up the phone and started dialing. "What was it I picked up from the floor of that room next door?"

188

"A dust puff?"

"That's what I said it was. I was wrong. What else could it have been?"

"Cotton," Ed said. "A puff of cotton from the packing?"

Ironside was talking on the phone again. He was speaking with Mrs. Alcorn, Tuck's secretary, and asking for Tuck's phone number in the city. He listened, then said he would like to see Tuck that evening and asked Mrs. Alcorn to find out if he would be available.

Waiting again, Ironside covered the mouthpiece of the phone and turned to Ed, Eve, and Mark. "He's back at the castle," he said. "He's tied up in conference with Tournabeau, but she's going to contact him on the intercom."

"Whee!" Mark said dryly.

"You're enjoying yourself a little too much," Eve told Ironside. "There's something almost sadistic about it."

Mrs. Alcorn was back on the line. Mr. Tuck would be happy to see Chief Ironside at any time he arrived, she said. Mr. Tuck would be at the castle the rest of the night.

Ironside thanked her, hung up, and began dialing once more.

"Let's see, to whom hasn't he talked yet?" Eve wondered.

"Alver Halverson," Mark said.

"Hello? Mr. Halverson?" Ironside said into the phone. "I want to ask a favor of you. Could you. . . ."

189

11 One Final Mistake

As SOON AS Ironside finished talking to Alver Halverson, he motioned to Ed, Eve, and Mark, then wheeled himself toward the door. They quickly got up from the table and hurried after him, looking at each other for a clue to this sudden development.

"Back to the castle?" Mark asked, opening the door for Ironside.

"Right. Back to the castle. Tuck will be there. And I think Tournabeau will be with him."

They reached the elevator.

"But to Halverson's first?" Ed asked. "I got the impression from what you said that you told him we'd pick him up."

"Everybody's right about everything all of a sudden," Ironside said. "I hope that's a good sign."

"Why Halverson?" Eve asked as the car reached the main floor.

"Because we may need him tonight — and on a moment's notice — to identify a painting or a number of paintings," Ironside replied, wheeling his way toward the exit.

"You know where the paintings are!" Ed exclaimed.

Ironside shook his head. "No, unfortunately, I don't. But I think Tuck does. And I have great hopes that he'll tell us where they are."

They reached the paddy wagon.

"Are you going to explain any of this to us?" Eve asked.

"While we're on the way," Ironside replied, gesturing for Mark to lower the lift.

When they reached the gallery a few minutes later, Ironside sent Ed in to get Alver Halverson. The art expert had apparently been waiting just inside the entrance, for Ed reappeared after only a few seconds, and Halverson was with him. Halverson looked baffled.

"Our adversary is an extremely clever man," Ironside told him as the van pulled away, headed for the Tuck estate. "I think he can put his hands on both kinds of paintings tonight — the real thing and fakes. Now, I

191

don't know the difference. That's why I need someone along who does."

"Yes, I understand that." Halverson nodded. "But, to tell you the truth, it is the *only* thing I understand about this. Do you know where the stolen paintings are?"

"Not exactly," Ironside admitted.

"Not exactly? Either you know or you do not know."

"All right, I don't know," Ironside replied. "But if everything goes right for me, Tuck will tell me where the paintings are."

Halverson shook his head. "I still do not understand."

"Welcome to the club," Eve said.

"The thing is, I think I know *how* the paintings were stolen," Ironside said. "And that, in turn, tells me *who*."

"The who, I assume, is Tuck," Ed said. "But would you mind filling us in on the how?"

"Be glad to." Ironside smiled. "It came to me all of a sudden — when Mark referred to the castle as a maze. What is a maze? It's a place where you're lost because everything looks the same. And that's a very apt description of that corridor in the castle."

"A particular corridor?" Halverson asked.

"Where the room is in which the paintings were crated," Ironside replied. He then addressed himself to Ed and Eve. "Remember when we were in that corridor and Mark got confused about which door led to the room?"

They nodded.

"My guess is that the same thing happened to Buckley

192

and Jones," Ironside said. "Now do you understand how it was done?"

Ed and Eve looked at each other, then faced back to Ironside, shaking their heads.

"All right, let's take it from the top," he said. "Let's assume that David Tuck wanted to steal his own paintings. He —"

"But —" Eve started to break in.

"Forget about motive for the moment," Ironside said. "Just take my word for it that he did. Then assume further that prior to the time Buckley and Jones arrived to pack the paintings and take them to the auction house, Tuck put together fifty-seven crates and placed them in the room that is next to the room in which they would be working."

"Just crates?" Ed asked.

"Just crates. Empty crates. Although, on second thought, I guess it wasn't that simple. The crates had to look pretty much like the crates that Buckley and Jones would put together later."

"How could he build something to look like something that hadn't been built yet?" Eve asked.

Ironside turned to Halverson. "Yes or no?"

"Well, yes," Halverson replied. "The crates all look pretty much alike. Unless one suspected something and examined them very closely, they would probably look the same."

"Objection withdrawn," Eve said.

"To continue," Ironside said, "Tuck built the crates,

193

just as he would have built them if he really intended them to hold valuable paintings, and he put them in the room next to the room in which Buckley and Jones would be working. He could control this, you understand, because he intended to take charge."

"Suppose it hadn't worked out that way," Ed suggested. "Suppose they —"

"He wasn't worried about that. Workmen for auction houses don't argue with millionaires who own castles."

"I suppose not."

"Now, Buckley and Jones arrive," Ironside went on. "Tuck takes them to the room they're to use, then stands by, directing, while they crate the fifty-seven paintings. So far, so good — for him. Next he takes them up to his office and has them sign the receipt. After that he takes them back to where they've come from — except that he doesn't. Instead he takes them to the room *next* to the room in which they've been working. Is this becoming clear now?"

"Jones did say that he started to go into a different room," Eve said.

"He started to go right back to where he'd been," Ironside said, "but Tuck detoured him and took him into the room next door. That room looked exactly like the room they'd actually worked in, so they assumed that it *was* the room."

"And they carried out the empty crates and put them into the truck," Ed said.

"Right."

194

"Do you mean the paintings were never on the truck?" Halverson asked.

"Never," Ironside replied. "They were left right where Buckley and Jones had crated them."

"Chief," Eve said, "what proof do we have of this?"

"Remember that puff of dust I found?"

"Yes."

"It wasn't. Wasn't dust, I mean. It was cotton. Cotton was used in padding the paintings, so Tuck would have used it in making up the empty crates. He missed a puff of it when he was cleaning up later — and I found it."

"And discarded it," Ed pointed out.

Ironside shrugged. "I won't need it. That wasn't the only clue. There was the chip out of the frame, too."

"Yes." Ed nodded. "The frame of the door of the empty room."

"When I got Buckley to shake up his brains," Ironside said, "he remembered that Jones had hit the frame of the door of the room and knocked a chip out of it. And which room was it?"

"The room next door," Eve said, "which proves that Buckley and Jones left the castle with the empty crates."

"Exactly."

"In other words," Ed said, "our evidence consists of a puff of cotton — which we don't have — and a chip in a doorframe."

"If you put it that way, it doesn't sound so good," Ironside admitted. "But I'm convinced that's the way it happened."

"The chip in the doorframe is fairly good evidence — along with Buckley's and Jones's testimony," Eve said.

Ironside snorted. "Given fifteen minutes to work at it, Tuck could have chips out of every doorframe in that castle," he said.

"I was trying to be helpful."

"The fact is that if I can't get Tuck to admit that he stage-managed the theft, I'm almost nowhere," Ironside said. "Either that or catch him with the paintings."

"Do you have *any* idea what he might have done with them?" Halverson asked.

"They're probably in the castle somewhere."

"We searched it thoroughly," Ed reminded him.

"Well, they're somewhere. . . ."

"Chief," Eve said, "you put me off when I mentioned it before, but — Well, what motive would Tuck have?"

"He thinks the paintings are fakes."

"Why?"

"Because he bought them from a man who was trying to fleece him, and he thinks he bribed Alver Halverson to authenticate them. To Tuck, who makes a business of outsmarting people who are trying to outsmart him, that adds up to one thing — fake paintings."

"Then he really is in trouble financially?" Eve asked.

"Apparently so," Ironside replied. "Otherwise, he wouldn't have been under such pressure to get a big price for the paintings."

"Let's go back a couple of steps," Ed said. "If this happened the way you think it did, Chief, and if Tuck

196

really thinks those paintings were fakes, why would he keep them?"

Ironside looked suddenly pained. "I hope you're wrong," he said.

"About what?" Eve asked.

"Ed has just pointed out that it's very likely Tuck has destroyed those paintings."

"No, no," Halverson said, concerned. "Those magnificent paintings? No, he could not do a thing like that! That would be . . . it would be barbaric!"

"Not if he thought they were fakes," Ironside said. "In fact, thinking that, he'd be foolish not to destroy them. Unless —" He thought for a moment, then went on. "Unless he hoped at some future time to get double duty out of them," he said.

"You've lost me again," Ed said.

"I'm trying to think the way Tuck thinks," Ironside said. "For one thing, we know that he depends a great deal on appearances. He told us that himself. We know, for instance, that he lives in that castle not because he happens to like castles, but because it makes him stand out; it makes him look like money. He collects paintings for the same reason, I think. The castle . . . the paintings . . . they're background, there to make Tuck look like a bigger and richer man than he actually is. It allows him to get more money, more easily, on which to operate."

"And he left that room in which the paintings were crated in disorder, too," Eve said. "That was for our

197

benefit, I think, and it worked, too, for a while."

"Right," Ironside said. "The presence of that debris made us concentrate on that room or, to put it another way, kept us from thinking about the *other* rooms — all of which substantiates my contention that he puts his faith in appearances. Okay? Now, suppose he has these paintings, which he assumes are fakes but which have been authenticated by a man with an impeccable reputation. He has already figured out one way to make money on them — by stealing them himself and collecting the insurance. What will he do with them now? Destroy them? Not if he can see a way to make more money on them."

"Yes, but how?" Ed asked.

"Let's say that ten years have passed. All that is known about the paintings is that they were authenticated and they were stolen. Suddenly they appear again — not on the public market, but on the black market. A man, working quickly, could sell them for a great deal of money. The reputation of the paintings would sell them." He turned to Halverson. "Isn't that right?"

"Very likely." Halverson nodded.

"It would be Tuck using appearances again," Ironside said.

Ed looked unconvinced. "If I came up with a theory like that," he said, "do you know what would happen to me?"

"It'd get a hearing," Ironside said, scowling.

"Then what?"

"Then I'd tell you that you needed a good rest."

"If anybody is interested in my opinion," Eve said, "I think the theory is right — but only up to a point. I can't see Tuck keeping the evidence around. It wouldn't be the smart thing to do. And Tuck prides himself on being smart."

"Who is the one person who could outsmart a man who prides himself on outsmarting others?" Ironside asked.

He got blank looks.

"Himself," he explained. "It wouldn't be the first time an outsmarter outsmarted himself."

Ed shook his head. "I'm with Eve. I'll go along with you. I think Tuck probably staged the theft — and that he did it the way you say he did. But I'll bet he got rid of those paintings as fast as possible."

"That would be criminal!" Halverson protested.

The others looked at him.

"That's why the police are interested," Ironside said.

"I don't mean criminal in that way, in a legal sense. I mean criminal in a moral way. To destroy masterpieces like that would be . . . would be . . . there is no word for it."

"Let's hope it hasn't happened," Ironside said, looking uneasy.

"Don't forget, it would be a mistake if he has destroyed them," Eve said to Halverson. "He thought they were fakes."

199

"That is no excuse!"

"Let's think," Ed said. "If they weren't destroyed, where are they? We went through all the rooms they could have been in."

"There are other places in that castle," Ironside pointed out.

Mark called back from the front seat. "You better do that thinking fast," he said. "We're almost there."

A few minutes later they reached the gate, then drove into the estate.

"Mr. Halverson," Ironside said, "I know how you feel about Tuck, but please try to keep it from showing. I'd like to keep this as pleasant as possible, at least until I'm ready to advise him that we know how he managed the theft."

"It will not be easy," Halverson said irritably. "Just thinking about the man disturbs me."

"Do your best," Ironside said gently.

When they got to the castle the caretaker was waiting for them at the entrance. He told them that Tuck was expecting them in his office.

"How do you plan to handle it?" Ed asked Ironside as the elevator ascended.

"Well, I hope. Otherwise I have no particular plan in mind. Any suggestions?"

"With what you have to go on, I think you'd better fall back on police brutality," Mark said.

The elevator door opened, and they got off and moved down the corridor toward the office.

"What do you make of these?" Ironside said to Halverson, indicating the inexpensive paintings along the corridor.

"For what they are, they are . . . well, they are what they are," Halverson replied. "I would not care to look at them very often. These things are turned out by mass-production methods. There is no genius represented here — only mediocre talent, if that."

"I rather like them," Ironside said.

"If I were a policeman, I might like them, too."

"Doesn't that remark —"

"I apologize," Halverson said. "But painting is very important to me, Chief. I am a snob about it, I know. It is the way I am."

"Here we are," Ironside said, indicating the door to Tuck's office. "Please, try to keep your feelings under control."

Mark opened the door that led into the outer office, and the others entered. Mrs. Alcorn had evidently gone for the day. At any rate she was not present.

Ed opened the next door, and the others passed by him, moving into Tuck's private office. Tuck was at his desk, with Tournabeau seated in an easy chair near it. They both rose as Ironside and his party entered the room. Tuck, smiling amiably, came forward. Tournabeau, looking somewhat sour, straggled after him.

Tuck greeted them all, then introduced Tournabeau to Alver Halverson. Then, turning to Ironside, he said, "Evidently this is an official call, Chief. I assume that

202

Alver is here for some reason other than his great admiration for me."

Ironside smiled. "Well, that has a lot to do with it," he replied. "But you're right; there is another reason for it." He faced toward Tournabeau. "I was surprised to hear that you had swallowed your pride and rejoined Mr. Tuck," he said.

"It wasn't a matter of swallowing my pride," Tournabeau replied crisply. "Dave asked me to come back. He practically begged me."

Tuck chuckled.

"I would say that begged is the right word," Tournabeau said sharply. "Wouldn't you, Dave?" His eyes, staring at Tuck, were cold and steady.

"Well —" Tuck shrugged — "I suppose you could say that."

"I would very much like to hear *you* say it," Tournabeau prodded.

Tuck looked at him warningly, then focused his attention on Ironside again. "If this is an official call, does it mean that you've caught the men who stole my paintings?" he asked.

"Man," Ironside corrected.

Tuck lifted his eyebrows. "Oh? You do know who did it?"

"Of course." Ironside smiled. "It was simply a matter of examining all the details very thoroughly. You, if anyone, should have realized that, Mr. Tuck."

Tuck frowned. "Why the reference to me?"

"Mr. Tuck, let's not be cute with each other anymore. You're my thief. I know it, and you — quite obviously — know it."

Tuck looked at Ironside evenly for a moment without changing expression; then, abruptly, he grinned. "I know it's a joke," he said. "I don't quite understand the humor of it, but I'm sure it's a joke."

Ironside shook his head.

Frowning again, Tuck said, "Chief, those paintings were on a truck and on their way to the city when they disappeared. How could I possibly have done it?"

Once more Ironside shook his head.

"Well, I'm afraid you'll have to explain it to me," Tuck said, looking baffled.

"Gladly," Ironside replied. He gestured toward the exit. "Shall we return to the scene of the crime?"

"Very well," Tuck said. "But I'm afraid you'll have to lead the way."

Ironside wheeled himself toward the door. Mark moved ahead to open it. Then the others followed. They passed through the outer office, proceeded down the corridor to the elevator, and descended. When they reached the floor where the paintings had been crated, Ironside took the lead again.

"Do any of these paintings interest you any more than the first ones you saw?" he said to Alver Halverson.

The gallery owner glanced at the painting he was passing. "Hardly," he replied.

"A couple of them aren't even signed," Ironside said.

204

"That's unusual. Even the worst painters like to claim their own works."

They reached the room where the paintings had been packed. Then, choosing his words very carefully, Ironside explained how Tuck had arranged to trick Buckley and Jones into taking empty crates while he kept the paintings.

"Fascinating." Tuck chuckled. "If I didn't know it was all fiction, Chief, I might actually believe it. Frankly, it sounds quite logical to me."

"I'm glad that you agree that it's possible," Ironside said.

"Oh, yes. However, won't you need some proof? A jury might agree, too, that it could have happened that way. But would a jury be satisfied simply to take your word for it?"

Ironside then told about finding the puff of cotton and the chip out of the doorframe, and about Buckley's story that the frame had been damaged by a crate.

Tuck laughed again. He entered the room where the paintings had been crated and picked up a piece of leftover board, then moved to the doorway and hit the frame with the length of lumber, taking a chip out of it.

"There, now, we have a chip out of this door, too," he said. "That proves conclusively that your whole theory was completely false, Chief."

"I have a number of witnesses to what you just did," Ironside said.

"Chief, be honest with me! Do you really believe you

205

could get a jury to convict me when you have so little evidence? A chip out of a doorframe!" he said derisively. "You're running a bluff. That's obvious. But the trouble is that you've picked the wrong man. I did not steal those paintings."

"We'll have to leave it up to that jury," Ironside said. "I'm convinced that you did."

"And my reason?" Tuck asked.

"Your motive? You needed money. You needed money fast."

"I could have got more money — and faster — by keeping the paintings and putting them up for sale. That's common knowledge." He pointed to Halverson. "Ask Alver. He'll tell you that."

"What you just said is very true," Ironside replied. "But you didn't know it. You probably still don't."

"You're talking nonsense," Tuck snapped.

"Just a minute," Tournabeau said, stepping forward. "What did you mean by that — that he didn't know it and probably still doesn't know it?"

"Mr. Tuck thought the paintings were fakes," Ironside explained. "You thought they were fakes, too."

Tournabeau looked like a man who had walked into a trap. "I . . . ah . . . I said that once," he admitted, "but . . . I . . . I didn't actually mean it. Of course they weren't fakes. They . . . ah. . . . But what I'm interested in knowing is —"

"Maybe I can help you out," Ironside interrupted. "It's fairly simple. Thinking that the paintings were fakes — and needing cash quickly — Mr. Tuck stole the paintings. He did it to get the insurance money. What he didn't realize was that he had outsmarted himself, because the paintings are, in fact, genuine."

Tournabeau glanced toward Halverson.

"No, you were wrong about that, too," Ironside said. "Mr. Tuck did not bribe Mr. Halverson to authenticate what were fake paintings. He thought he did. But the truth is that Mr. Halverson found those paintings to be, as I said before, genuine — the real goods."

Tournabeau whipped around to Tuck. "You —!"

"Just one moment!" Tuck said sharply, silencing him. "Think!" Then, cordial again, he turned once more to Ironside. "Chief," he said, "I think you're right. We will have to leave this up to a jury — that is, if you're going to be foolish enough to charge me when you have so little to go on."

"It isn't *that* little."

"Do you intend to arrest me? If you do, I'll go now and get in touch with my lawyer."

Ironside sighed. "No, I don't intend to arrest you. I don't have enough evidence — yet. But I'll get it. Sooner or later, I'll get it, Tuck."

Tuck's good humor returned completely. He chuckled again. "When you get the evidence, I hope you'll give me a little more warning than you gave me this time," he said. "That was a bit of a shock, springing it on me right out of the blue like that. Fortunately, I'm . . . uh, used to surprises. So I'm not often surprised anymore."

207

"You're fortunate," Ironside replied. He looked at Tournabeau. "You don't get on quite that well with the unexpected, do you?" he said. "You need more practice, apparently." Then, turning his chair, he wheeled himself back toward the elevator.

"Do you have time to stay for a late snack?" Tuck asked, following Ironside.

"He's busy," Tournabeau said rudely.

"I repeat the invitation," Tuck said to Ironside.

"Thank you, no. I'm not very good company when I've just suffered a defeat. I think I'll go home and brood."

Tuck laughed. "I doubt that."

Ironside suddenly halted. He studied the painting hanging near where he had stopped. "I noticed this before," he said. "This one isn't signed."

"I explained that to you," Tuck said. "They're inexpensive paintings. I buy them in large quantities." He addressed Halverson. "They're almost worthless, aren't they, Alver?"

"Yes," Halverson agreed. "Even worse than worthless. They are bad art."

"Are you a good winner, Mr. Tuck?" Ironside asked.

"I would hope so."

"Since you've beat me on this, I'd like to have a souvenir of the case." He pointed. "That painting would do nicely," he said.

"Let me send you a good painting — something of value," Tuck said.

208

"No. I couldn't accept anything like that. It would have to be something worthless. And. . . ." He smiled. "I've taken rather a liking to that painting."

"Very well," Tuck said. "If that's the painting you want, that's the painting you'll have. I'll have it delivered to you tomorrow."

"I wouldn't want you to have to go to that trouble," Ironside said. "I'll take it with me."

"It might get damaged," Tournabeau said, moving closer. "Paintings have to be handled just so."

"If it's worthless, what difference will it make?" Ironside shrugged. He spoke to Mark. "Get it for me, will you, please? We can take it in the van with us."

Mark moved to take the picture from the wall.

"You don't want that!" Tournabeau said sharply to Ironside.

Tuck, in almost the same tone, then addressed Tournabeau. "If that is the painting he wants, that's the painting he'll have," he said.

"Is something wrong?" Ironside asked innocently.

Mark had taken the painting from the wall.

"Don't —" Tuck began, speaking to Tournabeau again.

But he was too late. Tournabeau had put a hand inside his jacket. Now he was holding a gun on Ironside.

"That painting stays!" Tournabeau insisted.

Ironside turned to Tuck. "Mr. Tournabeau is probably not your first mistake," he said, "but he is obviously your worst."

Tuck nodded sadly. He looked at Tournabeau. "You fool!" he said. He faced back to Ironside. "If he had simply let you take the painting, would you have checked it at all?"

"Probably not," Ironside replied. "I would have assumed that it was really worthless, and I'd have stuck it in a corner somewhere and never looked at it again."

"Do you see now what you did?" Tuck asked Tournabeau. His tone, in defeat, was almost gentle.

"What does it matter?" Tournabeau retorted. "Who cares about your business? I want the money."

"They are *my* paintings," Tuck reminded him.

"No longer," Tournabeau said. He gestured with the gun. "Get over there with Halverson," he ordered Tuck. "As far as I'm concerned, you're one of them."

Grudgingly, Tuck moved.

"What exactly is the plan?" Ironside asked Tournabeau. "Off to Mexico? Or Europe? Or where?"

"I won't have to go that far to sell these paintings," Tournabeau replied. "Not now, now that I know they're genuine. I'll take them out of the frames and roll them up and — Never mind what I'll do." He waved the gun in Mark's direction. "Hand that over," he commanded, indicating the painting.

Mark looked at Ironside.

"Give it to him," Ironside said.

Holding the painting flat, Mark handed it toward Tournabeau. But when Tournabeau reached out for it, Mark brought the frame down hard, hitting him on the

210

gun hand. The pistol clattered to the floor. Ed scooped it up.

"That was a fool trick!" Ironside snapped at Mark. "He could have killed you!"

"You said to give it to him." Mark grinned.

"I meant — Oh, well. . . ." He turned to Tuck. "Do you intend to carry on the charade?" he asked. "Or will you show us where the other paintings are?"

"You win, Chief. The paintings are all over the castle, hidden behind inexpensive paintings just like this one."

"Take Tournabeau down to the paddy wagon," Ironside said to Ed. "Mr. Tuck and I have some collecting to do."

As Ironside and Tuck made the rounds, removing valuable canvases from behind worthless canvases, Ironside asked, "Was Tournabeau blackmailing you? Is that why you took him back?"

"Yes. He figured out where I'd put the paintings. He didn't know, however, how I'd stolen them — until you explained it to him a while ago."

"Do you know what tripped you up?"

"Yes, a detail," Tuck replied. "I had to cut some of the inexpensive paintings down to make them fit the frames. Unfortunately, in doing the cutting, I shaved off some of the signatures."

"Right. That's how I spotted it."

"What really distresses me is that it was all unnecessary," Tuck said. "I could have sold these paintings at

211

auction and got the money I needed. But I really thought they were fakes."

"That's the difference between us," Ironside said.

"Pardon?"

"I've been told that we're a lot alike," Ironside explained. "I just discovered the difference — an important difference. I haven't reached the point where I believe that everything and everyone, despite the evidence, is a fake."

Tuck glanced at him. "I guess you are fortunate."

"Fortunate but poor."

"And I am rich and on my way to prison."

"Some days, life's like that," Ironside said consolingly.

Whitman ADVENTURE and MYSTERY Books

SPORTS STORIES
Throw the Long Bomb!
Hot Rod Road

THE POWER BOYS
The Burning Ocean
The Vanishing Lady
The Million-Dollar Penny

ADVENTURE TALES
Tarzan of the Apes
The Return of Tarzan
Tarzan and the City
of Gold
Tarzan and the Lost Safari
The Space Eagle
. . . .
Walt Disney
The Gnome-Mobile
Blackbeard's Ghost

TELEVISION FAVORITES
Bonanza
Killer Lion
Treachery Trail

Garrison's Gorillas

Lassie
Secret of Smelters' Cave
Secret of the Summer
Bristlecone Pine
Wild Mountain Trail

The Monkees

Rat Patrol

Star Trek

Man From U.N.C.L.E.
Gunrunners' Gold
Gentle Saboteur

I Spy

F Troop

The Invaders

The Big Valley